Rain of Terror

Mark Phillips

First Printing

Mark Phillips

www.rainofterror.com

1-866-867-3407

ISBN-13: 978-0615511016
ISBN: 0615511016

Cover Design by Mark Phillips
Typesetting by Mark Phillips

Photography Credit
Storm in Field:FOX News Latino: Pix-of-the-week-13 20.jpg
Free Desktop Rain On Windshield from
http://www.pulsardesktop.eu
Virus: Alex Roznichenko 2004

PRINTED IN THE UNITED STATES OF AMERICA

Kindle Version : http://www.amazon.com/dp/B005AWQ7UA

About the Author

Mark Phillips lives with his dear wife Lois in Plains, Georgia. Mark is the father of seven children, Janelle, Bronson, Graydon, Carrie, Leighton, Alyssa and Tamma. He began by telling stories to his children and they encouraged him to write a book.

Dedication

This book, my first novel, is dedicated to my children. Without their motivation and encouragement to finish the book, this work would still be sitting on my old computer hard drive.

Appreciation

Thank you to my wife Lois for her excellent eye for detail. Her help in the final edit made all the difference.

Thank you to the Lord Jesus Christ my Savior for saving my soul. He is the one who has blessed me with any creativity and writing talent I might have.

Chapter 1

The darkness of space was interrupted by a brilliant flash as the ancient meteor passed close to the rings of Saturn. For untold years the one hundred ton behemoth had been on the same course, diminished not in the least by the vacuum of space, or the distance it had traveled. It had passed by hundreds of solar systems, planets and suns, not concerned in the least with the beauty being displayed.

The collision of this massive lump of ice with the smaller meteorites in Saturn's orbit caused a splash of millions of ice crystals to expand out from the impact. Its beauty ethereal, fragments displaying all the colors of the rainbow.

Its passage, however, not slowed in the least. The meteor's trajectory was changed, not by the impact, but by the proximity to Saturn itself. The gravitational pull had its effect on the meteor and its path was changed infinitesimally, though just enough.

2 MARK PHILLIPS

Chapter 2

Phoenicians cooking on sand discovered glass around 3500 BC, but it took about 5,000 years more for glass to be shaped into a lens for the first telescope.. The telescope was introduced to astronomy in 1609 by the great Italian scientist Galileo Galilei, who became the first man to see the craters of the moon, and who went on to discover sunspots, the four large moons of Jupiter, and the rings of Saturn. Galileo's telescope was similar to a pair of opera glasses in that it used an arrangement of glass lenses to magnify objects. This arrangement provided limited magnification and Galileo could see no more than a quarter of the moon's face without repositioning his telescope.

In 1704, Sir Isaac Newton announced a new concept in telescope design whereby instead of glass lenses, a curved mirror was used to gather in light and reflect it back to a point of focus. This reflecting mirror acted like a light-collecting bucket: the bigger the bucket, the more light it could collect. The reflector telescope that Newton designed opened the door to magnifying objects millions of times, far beyond what could ever be obtained with a lens.

Newton's fundamental principle of using a single curved mirror to gather in light remained the same. The major change that took place was the growth in the size of the reflecting mirror, from the 6-inch mirror used by Newton to the 6-meter (236 inches in diameter) mirror of the Special Astrophysical Observatory in Russia, which opened in 1974.

Organizations arose over the years which specialized in observing the cosmos. The foremost of them, the European Southern Observatory (ESO) is an intergovernmental, European organization for astronomical research. It has ten member countries: Belgium, Denmark, France, Germany, Italy, the Netherlands, Portugal, Sweden, Switzerland and United Kingdom. ESO operates astronomical observatories in La Silla, Chile and has its headquarters in Garching, near Munich, Germany. The Very Large Telescope (VLT) on Paranal is located on a 2600 m high mountain some 130 km south of Antofagasta.

The ESO Very Large Telescope (VLT) at the Paranal Observatory (Atacama, Chile) is the world's largest and most advanced optical telescope. It comprises four 8.2-m reflecting Unit Telescopes and several moving 1.8-m Auxiliary Telescopes, the light beams of which can be combined in the VLT Interferometer (VLTI).

With its unprecedented optical resolution and unsurpassed surface area, the VLT produces extremely sharp images and can record light from the faintest and most remote objects in the Universe.

All four telescopes and five large state-of-the-art multi-mode astronomical instruments are now in operation. The telescopes were named ANTU-The Sun, KUEYEN-The Moon, MELIPAL-The Southern Cross and YEPUN-Venus. When working together they are one of the most powerful, and accurate telescopes in the world.

62 year old Frederick Schoefield, the Director of ESO - Paranal, harrumphed into his mouthpiece. "Don't be ridiculous! That is *very* unlikely, if not impossible for this

to go undetected before now. It must be a sensor alignment malfunction."

His balding pate and thin mustache, bifocal wire rimmed glasses and polka dot bow tie gave the impression that he was an academic with little time for reality. Although this was quite accurate, not many knew that beneath the lab coat and his polyester trousers he wore Mickey Mouse boxers. His secret love for all things Disney was only known by his late wife and went with her to the grave. It belied a sense of fun and a sense of humor that only his closest friends ever saw. To his colleagues he was the consummate professional.

Derek Manheim was in the computer lab on the other end of the phone, trying to convince Frederick of the validity of what he saw.

Derek was in his early thirties but still considered young by his peers. It didn't help too much that he kept his blond hair swept back in a ponytail, his sideburns long and his blue jeans holey. He raced through life at a pace fueled by Starbucks coffee and Skittles. Completing his Masters and PhD at the University of Hawaii at Manoa in four years was a record that had yet to be broken.

Derek had always loved the stars and the mystery that deepened the further one saw, the less one knew. It amazed him that just when man thought he'd reached the end of the universe another more beautiful layer was revealed. In the seemingly infinite universe our world seemed microscopic by comparison.

As a young boy Derek read all he could on astronomy, the zodiac, and geology trying to figure out how it all worked together. He would spend hours with a reference book, a red lense flashlight and ever stronger telescopes out in the field behind his Iowa home.

Derek's parents tolerated his 'hobby', not understanding that he could actually earn a living gazing at the stars. They were hard working farmers from a family of hard working farmers who settled Iowa in the 1860s. As the oldest son with two sisters he was expected to continue the tradition and the family business.

Derek however had no interest in farming. His sights were set much, much higher. Eventually his parents realized that no matter their persistence, Derek wasn't going to change his mind. When he graduated High School with honors and a scholarship to any college in the USA, they resigned themselves to giving their family business to their eldest daughter. Christa had always wanted the farm and had learned more from her father about running a farm then most sons would have.

Derek continued his conversation with Frederick, gesturing animatedly, and striding back and forth as he spoke through the wireless telephone in his ear.

"Frederick, I am absolutely certain. It just appeared! Come see for yourself, if you don't believe me!" As the Head of Student Research, his opinions were often disregarded as inexperienced or over-enthusiastic nonsense, despite his ability to out think his seniors. Derek had explained to Frederick, that he had found a shadow on the rings of Saturn, followed briefly by a flash of light. It was an unexpected and previously undocumented occurrence. Something large, maybe a meteor, had collided with the rings of Saturn! This time he was definitely on to something. "You must come and have a look. I am not making this up!"

"That's what you said when you found the pyramid orbiting Mars!" Laughing to himself he continued in a much sterner voice than he really felt, "Now, I am a busy man with much to do. I expect ESO staff, *including* student researchers, to behave in a professional manner. Don't bother me again with your childish jokes." Frederick hung up the phone. He thought to himself that if it were such an important discovery, and not another fraud, Derek would persevere until the proof was absolute.

"I am not a Student Researcher, I am the head of the department!" Derek yelled to dead air. Derek couldn't believe it! He finally found something *real* and worth investigating and his pyramid prank had come back to haunt him.

It was three years ago. Couldn't he ever get past the childish stunt? Derek had digitally enhanced the photo of Mars from the Antu telescope to show an orbiting pyramid, complete with scars from asteroid hits. It took him hours to perfect the image. He supposed that because Frederick initially was taken in by the fraud, and was later embarrassed by it, that he was particularly sensitive now.

However, this image was not digitally enhanced. It was not a fraud. The event needed to be verified. If it was indeed a meteor, based on the size of its shadow, it could be a risk to Earth. Not since man had made the first telescope had an event of this magnitude been recorded. The data from the telescope was now recorded and stored in the massive computer complex built into the mountain.

After a quick analysis of the data Derek was convinced himself. Now he had to convince Frederick, even if it took all night. He sat down at the computer console again, and entered his password. ARMAGEDDON.

Little did he know how ironic his choice of password would become.

Chapter 3

Melinda Chase liked Atlanta, Georgia. Atlantans are fiercely proud of their city. They bubble over with enthusiasm for Braves baseball, Hawks basketball, Thrashers hockey and Falcons football. The city has hosted two Super Bowls.

News of Atlanta's special formula for friendliness combined with pride emerged during the 1996 Olympics, when the city opened its doors and made the world feel welcome.

Downtown Atlanta has several hubs of activity: the World Congress Convention Center; CNN Center, home of Ted Turner's 24-hour Cable News Network; and Peachtree Center, a combination of grand hotels, upscale retail and modern businesses. Cultural events include a myriad of outdoors fairs, festivals and concerts.

Just a few miles away, the city's progressive sights and sounds evolve into quiet, dogwood- and azalea-lined streets. Residents of Atlanta's historic in-town neighborhoods enjoy restored homes, baby buggy-friendly sidewalks, unusual antique shops and art studios, and intimate, cozy outdoors cafes. The rolling hills and greenery mixed with high tech glass and chrome of the city was a nice mix.

Melinda would often take her lunch on the grounds of Emory University and today was no different. Melinda sat under a huge dogwood tree, sipped lemonade while listening to the cicadas whine to the summer heat like some kind of audio thermometer. The only thing that she didn't like about Atlanta was the cockroach. Somehow, she thought, as Director of the National Center for Infectious Diseases (NCID) a division of the Center for Disease Control (CDC) I should be able to figure out a way to obliterate these vermin from the world.

The best scientific minds could only manage a temporary eradication at best. Always, always, they came back like a plague from the Old Testament. Some said they came home in grocery bags. Some said they come in on fruit, or indoor plants. Melinda didn't care where they came from they were just disgusting. She could deal with Ebola, Escherichia Coli (E. Coli), even narcotizing fasciitis, but the creepy crawlers were another story.

"Time to get back!" thought Melinda as she folded up her napkin, her sandwich wrapper and her nylon lunch bag. After meticulously sweeping the crumbs off her skirt, she arose from the colorful blanket she had been sitting on and folded it neatly. Everything went into her carryall bag that matched her vanilla white business suit and she walked briskly in the direction of CDC.

Melinda entered through the main entrance. Security was tight since 9/11 and Melinda had to show her ID, and press her eye against a retinal scanner, just to get passed the front lobby. Then she needed her ID card to swipe the elevator controls to the top floor and finally a hand-print scanner to enter her wing of the building. "Meeting in five folks!" Melinda said as she strode purposefully through the offices of her team. This caused a whirlwind of activity as her team gathered documents, charts and notes together so they wouldn't be late. Melinda entered her office.

Tastefully decorated with just enough feminine accents, the room was all Melinda. She had her educational record on display on one wall and her pictures with celebrities and officials (including the President of the United States) on the other. The remaining wall held watercolors over a red leather couch, a chair and a glass coffee table with a vase of colorful flowers in its center.

Hers was one of the few offices with a view of the city and enough square footage to hold a meeting of up to ten people. Her custom-made, high gloss, cherry desk was a half-circle shape with her executive chair on the strait edge facing the room, its back to the window. Five people could sit comfortably around the desk facing Melinda with three more on the couch and one on the chair.

Melinda liked to be in control. This was what drove her passion for eliminating disease. She hated to think that there was a bug, a virus, or a toxin that she couldn't master. Recognized for her research and creative thinking Melinda used her desire for control over nature to drive her creativity with much success in her career. However, this same desire for control drove her husband Greg to divorce her.

It was not intentional on her part, but from his point of view she was critical and unforgiving. He tried to live up to her expectations and he submitted to her control of his life for three years because he loved her. At first it was cute when she told him what to do. Then it was almost easier just to let her be in control, make the decisions, handle the finances etc. In the end Greg's ego could take it no more.

Being high rise steel worker, Greg was often ridiculed by his workmates for being 'hen-pecked'. There was something about being a man that makes a man want to lead, to be in charge, to have the admiration of his wife for the decisions he makes, for his physical strength and protection. He had to escape for his own sanity.

Melinda missed the physical intimacy but she was glad he was gone. "He was such a wimp!" She thought. Although she could have used his help with Jessica, her seventeen year old daughter from her first marriage.

In high school and suffering all the peer pressure to conform into being a non-conformist had had its effect on Jessica. Caught between her controlling mother and her absent but loveable father, Jessica rebelled. From tattoos to body piercing, to blue hair to heavy-metal music, Jessica fit the profile of a rebellious youth.

Melinda sat behind her desk and gathered her notes and papers together whilst the team scrambled in.

Jacob Wettstien, the eldest of the team was the first in. A traditionalist he entered with a yellow legal pad and lead pencil in hand, nothing else. His gray hair was perfectly combed to one side. He wore a pair of navy blue polyester pants with a white long sleeve, open collared, dress shirt under the tan wool vest that he always wore.

Jacob was a fixture at CDC. He had survived three directors and was working on his fourth. Although he could just as easily cripple her career like he did the last joker, he liked Melinda and gave her every opportunity to succeed.

"Good afternoon Melinda. How was lunch?" he asked as he sat on her right. "Perfect, Jake! I love the peace of the University grounds." Melinda replied.

"Wonderful!" Jacob said. Jacob could run the department himself, and often filled in for Melinda, but didn't like the politics of the job. He would much rather be hands on when it came to problem solving rather than going to lunches and dinners with the 'elite' of Washington and Atlanta just to get funding. With his PHD in microbiology and his tenure he had more knowledge in his head than most computer databases.

Sam Smith was the next one to enter the room, followed immediately by Rhonda Lewis. The two were an "item". Everyone new it but they pretended not to notice. Despite the distractions of the young romance they were a good team.

"Hey" Sam said as he greeted Melinda and sat down with his PDA chirping. "Hey yourself" Melinda said in return. Rhonda just smiled and sat beside Sam. They were together responsible for computer tracking and mapping of virus outbreaks around the world. If there was anything going on, they knew it.

Jacob looked at Sam with a sigh. Sam was a tall and skinny young man who looked every bit like a high school nerd. Although these days being a nerd was cool. He kept his black hair in the latest hair style, of 'no style', which is what Jacobs generation would have called a 'bed head' and irritated him immensely. The 'Buddy Holly' glasses apparently were back in style as were the rolled up jeans. Jacob did have to admit the kid was bright.

Sam could "unofficially" get information from any computer source in the world. At 13 he was arrested for hacking into the FBI criminal files and changing the faces of the top ten most wanted to various dignitaries and celebrities, including number one - the President of the United States.

Recognizing his talent, the FBI recruited him to work for them, which he did for 10 years. He left them a year ago and came to work for CDC.

Melinda recruited him a short time after they met at a Braves game, where they shared a conversation and a hot dog, and concern for the environment.

Rhonda was a traditionally educated MIT graduate that was incredibly bright but not particularly intuitive when it came to thinking 'out of the box'. She was, however, a genius when it came to figuring out new algorithms necessary for forecasting the success of new antivirus.

Rhonda had bright red hair and kept it up all the time, either in a bun or a pony tail. She often wore ball caps or berets and most people wouldn't know how long it really was. She had a button nose as some people called it, freckles graced her cheeks and she had brilliant blue eyes that sparkled when she laughed.

Rhonda was a bit of an introvert due to the teasing in high school and college. This was both for her red hair and for her brains. When she graduated top of her class at MIT, a great many people stopped teasing her, particularly when they heard the salaries she was offered.

Noah Drew was the last one in. Big, black and beautiful is how they described the African American. He was handsome, well built, funny, and sensitive. This combined with his wealth from a dot-Com investment and a voice 'in the basement' made him more than attractive to most women. He had broken many hearts but he was completely oblivious to his effect on them.

His patients came first. His compassion as a doctor was tremendous and sometimes in an effort to save a life he drove himself beyond any reasonable limit.

Noah came from a famous family. His father, Charles Richard Drew, was the inventor of the blood bank. His introduction of a system for the storing of blood plasma revolutionized the medical profession.

Charles Drew first utilized his system on the battlefields of Europe and the Pacific during World War II. He later organized the world's first blood bank project - Blood for Britain. He also established the American Red Cross Blood Bank, of which he was the first director until his death in 1950.

Noah followed in his Canadian father's footsteps and entered the medical profession at an early age. Soon recognized in his own right as a skilled emergency medicine professional, Noah joined the CDC after leaving Johns Hopkins Medical Center seven years earlier.

Melinda depended on Noah's life saving skills many times in the past and he was indispensable to her. She had to admit she wasn't immune to his effect on women but kept it to herself. "Glad you could make it Noah" she said with a smile.

"I'm not late am I?" Noah asked.

"Not at all, Noah, Just saying 'hello'!"

"Great, Sorry" said Noah as he sat down clipboard in hand.

"Has anyone seen Charlotte?" Melinda asked looking out the door to her office.

With no response, she picked up her phone and buzzed the intercom system for Charlotte's phone. "Charlotte, Melinda here. Are you there?" she asked.

"*Yes, Melinda. How can I help you?*" Charlotte replied through the speaker.

"We are having a meeting, could you take notes please?"

"*Certainly, I'll be right there. Sorry I didn't know about it.*"

"That's OK. It's kind of impromptu."

"*All right, see you in a minute.*"

"Thanks Char."

"Ok, Sam why don't you get set up for the hotspot report while we're waiting." Melinda suggested.

"No problem" said Sam. He picked up his PDA which was wirelessly linked to the network server and called up the 3D holographic display in the centre of the table. The holo-transmitters were cleverly concealed in the ceiling.

The display showed the world in the form of a twenty inch globe suspended eight inches above the table. It was a beautiful representation of the 'blue planet' displaying the oceans, seas and lakes in vibrant blue, the greens of the forests, the blues of the mountains and the browns of the desert areas were all amazingly accurate. One could imagine oneself viewing the actual Earth from space.

Charlotte La Roche arrived and sat down, set her laptop in front of her. Charlotte was a petite brunette in a business suit with a trim figure on her five foot one frame. Hailing from the bayous of New Orleans and of Cajun background, she could sweet talk you out of a million dollars and you would thank her for the privilege. She nodded to Melinda, "Ready!"

"Ok, Sam bring us up to date."

"Switching to the hotspot color palette." Sam said as he used his PDA's stylus like a conductor would direct a symphony.

The globe changed from its pristine look, to one from a children's coloring book. The Continents and oceans were still visible, but the colors changed to green, yellow, orange and red areas. The oceans were still primarily blue, but had blue, light blue, light green and pink areas.

The highlighted areas represented the severity of any outbreak of virus, infectious disease or toxic poisoning. India, South America, and Africa represented the most 'colored' segments due to the fact that disease control was not quite up to standards in these continents as the governments that represented the many nations there squandered aid from the world's richest countries.

"Africa is the worst right now. The Mozambique government has managed to perform magic in that country with the UN medical supplies sent to them last month. According to my sources, over 3 million dollars in aid has disappeared without a trace. The Ecoli outbreak there is spreading and hundreds are dying each day. Latest statistics show over 3,000 dead, 1,300 in makeshift quarantine."

The map zoomed in to the African continent, the globe becoming a cube, with the same display on four sides.

"Here you can see Mozambique. The outbreak is confined to the southwestern region, but has spread to the neighboring countries. Two or three cases have been found in Malawi in a village called Phalombe. The authorities in Malawi have closed the border with Mozambique because of the danger of infection and are shooting anyone trying to cross. So far 13 have been killed. Only 1 was found to be infected."

"That's terrible! How can they get away with it?" asked Noah.

"Because they can. The UN has no authority in that country, and will not involve itself with minor skirmishes." Jacob advised.

"That's right and we cannot get involved unless invited to help. It's a dog's breakfast" said Melinda. "Let's keep going. What's the orange area in Chechnya Sam?"

The map changed to Eastern Europe and zoomed in on Chechnya. Sam explained.

"The orange area is a typhoid epidemic. It is getting under control now that winter is setting in. The cold helps to stop the spread. Mass graves were discovered near Botlikh and when they were dug up several people were infected. They in turn infected family members, coworkers and friends as is typical before containment. So far it has reached as far as Kirovauya and Sovetskoye, but if it reaches Groznyy they'll be in big trouble. The government there seems to have a good handle on containment however, and it should be downgraded in a day or two to level two, yellow."

Rhonda added "I've run the numbers and I don't think we have anything to worry about."

"Great, thanks guys" Melinda said then added, "OK Sam give me the bad news."

"Sure" replied Sam.

The map zoomed out and changed into a globe. It rotated and zoomed in on Iraq, and changed back into a cube again. The South East area of Iraq was red, bled into orange, yellow and green in a northward blend.

"What is going on there now? There was nothing there yesterday!" Rhonda commented.

"According to my sources, there were several biological weapons released there by Al-Qaeda terrorists last night in an attempt to get the US to pull out. Where they got them from I don't know, but they are real. No word yet on the chemical makeup of the bio-weapon, but according to the symptoms it looks like it carries an immune system suppression drug and an Ebola like virus. Death occurs within 48 hours. No body count yet. The US forces there were protected by their gear and only civilian deaths likely will result." Sam concluded.

"We haven't been contacted yet, but given the severity of the attack, we will be. I'll phone the Pentagon directly after this meeting. What's next Sam?" Melinda asked.

"Nothing of that severity," Sam changed the view again for each of the next outbreak zones. "India has a cholera epidemic in Karaikal province in the South East near Neravy due to the flooding from the monsoon season with resources on site and is designated an orange zone over 200 square miles. Mexico has been hit by Hurricane George, thousands are without shelter and sanitary conditions make Mexico City an orange zone."

"What is the UN doing as far as medical resources and supplies?" asked Noah.

"Aid organizations have mobilized and the Red Cross has set up food distributions and triage in India. As far as I know Mexico has not asked for help yet." Sam answered.

"I had a call today from our ambassador in Mexico City. He says he has been authorized by the President of

Mexico to request assistance from us to evaluate the situation. I received the OK from the State Department and have dispatched a team. They leave tomorrow morning." Melinda said.

"Great!" said Noah.

"Sam, see if you can get more info on Iraq." Melinda instructed. "Rhonda, see if you can extrapolate the spread of Cholera in India. I know we'll need it soon. Noah, contact the Red Cross and see how they are handling the load in Mexico. Jake, see if you can find out more from your contacts at the State Department, or anyone else you can think of regarding our Nation's response to the attack. I'll study the rest of your report Sam and see if we are needed anywhere else. That's it folks, let's get to it."

As they filed out, Melinda hoped that the scum that released the biological weapon in Iraq got a taste of their own medicine.

Chapter 4

The meteor on its new trajectory continued on its journey through space. Passing through the orbit of Mars, it continued on a collision course with earth. The proximity of the meteor to the Sun's radiation caused its brilliance to flare, making a comet tail visible with the naked eye from almost anywhere on the planet.

Chapter 5

Derek Manheim took another sip from his coffee. It was cold but still had the desired effect. He had been awake for 42 hours now and was determined to prove that the light display wasn't a malfunction of the billion dollar telescope. Skittle wrappers littered his desk and the floor around him.

"Come on!" He whispered to himself. "Come on, come on!" The computer beeped as if in reply, but not from the current program he was running. A background program message leapt to the foreground of his screen.

"UNKNOWN STELLAR BODY DETECTION

LOCATION: 3024 0335 0011

TIME CODE: 20041015:19:35:23:22:11

MASS: 123,117 tonnes

COURSE: 000 002 010

WARNING: Impact Pacific Ocean 49 Degrees North 270 Degrees West

ESTIMATED TIME OF IMPACT: 97 hours 42 minutes 39 seconds"

Derek sat and stared at the message. He tabbed quickly to the background program. "Verify" he typed. The computer responded:

"UNKNOWN STELLAR BODY DETECTION

LOCATION: 3024 0333 0000

TIME CODE: 20041015:19:37:31:17:00

MASS: 123,117 tonnes

COURSE: 000 002 010

WARNING: Impact Pacific Ocean 49 Degrees North 270 Degrees West

ESTIMATED TIME OF IMPACT: 97 hours 40 minutes 31 seconds

VERIFIED.

SEND ALERT NOTIFICATION??"

Derek thought for a minute and held his breath. "Crap!" he whispered. Derek typed "No" then went over to the computer interface to the VLTI telescope and punched in the coordinates of the mass.

He then went over to the wall size view screen and waited as the computer redirected the telescopes to the new coordinates. The screen changed slowly as hydraulic arms and massive gears took the computers instructions and made them into reality. A blurry white mass moved into the centre of the screen.

Derek switched on the computers audio interface and said. "KAMY, verify coordinates I entered - *3024 0333 0000*"

"Coordinates verified, Derek." the computer voice answered. KAMY was the name of the main computer system that controlled the telescopes. It stood for the VLTI telescopes at the facility - KUEYEN, ANTU, MELIPAL, and YEPUN. The computer used Artificial Intelligence to understand and answer verbal queries from Derek and other authorized users at the facility.

"Focus" Derek commanded. The blurry white mass quickly changed to a clearly defined meteor, its tail clearly visible to the left. "Print two copies full size with Alert information." He said and the color laser printer sprang to life.

Derek walked over to the printer and waited for the copies to come out. If this is the same meteor that flew through the rings of Saturn a few days ago, it must have tremendous velocity, he thought to himself. If it *is* the same one, I was right!

When the prints were complete Derek snatched them up and started towards the door. Before he could get there it opened and in marched Frederick Schoefield. "Derek, do you know who reset the telescopes? I was right in the middle of a project when the view changed to Haley's comet from 10 years ago. It looks like a simulation of some kind. Were you up to your tricks again?" asked Frederick.

"No. Listen Fred, this is not another hoax. Take a look at the time index. This is happening now! There is a meteor of tremendous mass on its way to Earth and it is moving fast!" Derek exclaimed.

"Unbelievable! Let me see the photos…. Hmm. This is incredible! Have you verified the data?" asked Frederick.

"Yes…" started Derek

"KAMY, verify all data related to current stellar body." commanded Frederick.

"Working… All data verified, Doctor Schoefield." the computer responded.

"My goodness! Have you alerted the ESONET?" asked Frederick

"Not yet. I wanted to show you first. However, we don't have much time at all. The impact is calculated in only four days. Depending on the makeup of the meteor it could create a tidal wave that would wipe out most major cities on the west coast all the way to Alaska."

"You're right Derek! We have to send an alert immediately. Government agencies around the world will need to be notified. Particularly the US, Canada and Japan will be effected. Send the alert immediately. I will start phoning my contacts at the US Department of Homeland Security and the Public Safety and Emergency Preparedness Canada. That should give them enough time to start evacuations. I hope they believe us!"

"They should! It is probably visible by the naked eye by now in some parts of the world." He paused. "KAMY, calculate the affect of an impact of this size to the ocean and the atmosphere and show us on the view screen." Derek commanded.

"WORKING…CALCULATIONS COMPLETE. CREATING GRAPHIC REPRESENTATION OF IMPACT AND EFFECT ON OCEAN AND ATMOSPHERE."

The view screen now showed a satellite image of the world overlooking the Pacific Ocean. The proposed impact was 500 miles off the coast of Vancouver, Canada. As the computer simulated the impact, a fireball raced through the atmosphere creating a fiery display of light and smoke. When it struck the ocean, a mushroom cloud rose like that of an atomic bomb, lifting water and steam miles into the atmosphere.

A wave of enormous proportions was sent out across the ocean in all directions like a ripple from a pebble in a pool. It was followed by another and another as the water rushed into the impact site to fill the whole created by the meteor and then was forced out again by the weight of its own mass. "The devastation will be fantastic, unbelievable." Frederick exclaimed.

Derek commanded, "KAMY send alert notification for this stellar body across ESONET. Use alert protocol one. Send copies to the heads of state of each country affected by an impact of this size."

"I am sorry Derek. You are not authorized for Alert Protocol One." The computer responded.

"KAMY, this is Frederick Schoefield, send alert notification protocol one as previously requested."

"Completed Dr. Schoefield." The computer responded officiously.

"Thank you KAMY"

"You are welcome Doctor."

"What do we do now Fred?" Derek asked.

"I guess you were right about Saturn, hmm? We keep on tracking the event until impact. No telling what might happen in the next few days to change its trajectory. Keep watch my friend, and good work! Now, I must go and make a few phone calls." Frederick answered and strode purposefully towards the door.

Derek sat down hard at his desk and blew out a slow breath, rubbed his eyes then scratched his head with both hands. He looked up at the ceiling. "KAMY, identify stellar body as M1, for Manheim One. Maintain focus on M1 and track position and trajectory until further notice. You are authorized to reposition all telescopes as necessary to maintain visual contact as long as possible. Block any requests to use the VLTI except by myself or Fred. Alert me if any major change occurs in the course of M1."

"Working..."

Completed, Derek."

"One more thing, scan M1 and determine the composition of the meteor. It looks too big to have such a small mass." Derek commanded.

"Working...Insufficient data to complete the request, Derek. Do you want me to continue scanning?" asked the computer.

"Yes, please. And let me know when you have any results. I'm going… to… get… some sleep."

"Scanning In Progress. Pleasant dreams!"

Derek, head on his arms was already snoring

Chapter 6

Classic Rock music blared from the hidden speakers of a state of the art stereo system. Led Zeppelin was inviting a trip in rocket ship while sweat poured off Matt Parker as he worked through his routine.

His feet and hands a blur as he struck the effigies of four men surrounding him. Like a dancer on steroids, Matt struck one then the other, moving gracefully, his balance sure, his concentration total.

With a final blow to the head of one of his attackers he landed on his feet with his guard up and ready for any surprise. With a final deep breath and eyes closed he assumed a relaxed stance. For a moment it seemed that he was in a trance, then he straightened and walked over to a bench, picked up a white towel and dried the perspiration from his face and neck.

He picked up a remote and suddenly the room was silent. After a drink from his water bottle, he threw the empty into the wastebasket across the room. It arced perfectly and clunked into its center. "Two points!" he exclaimed. "Yes!" like a teenager.

Matt Parker took his training seriously. After several years of training he had attained a black belt in Kick Boxing and a black belt in Defendo. At 37 years old, five feet eleven and 200 lbs he was all muscle but incredibly flexible. His dark hair and dark complexion were accented by his deep blue eyes.

His equipment was extensive. The universal gym was in one corner, free weights in another, whilst a running machine, a step machine and a total gym faced a mirrored wall.

In the center of the room was a training area complete with a punching bag and four life-like men used for his kickboxing routines. The outside wall was all glass and overlooked his kidney shaped pool..

Beyond his yard, the Limekiln Canyon and the Lexington Reservoir were in view just outside Los Gatos, California. The sun was just rising above the horizon and casting a pink glow across the country side.

Matt's house was a 3 million dollar beauty. At 4000 square feet it was built in a Spanish style with red clay brick roof, and appropriate arches and alcoves. With an exterior like a Casa Bella, the interior was completely modern and simply decorated. It had hardwood floors throughout and it had every convenience known to man. Matt had the perfect bachelor's pad.

Matt walked out of the workout room, through the hall to his bedroom where he stripped off his clothes and walked into his on suite bathroom. He passed by the Jacuzzi tub and entered the glass enclosed shower. Automatic vents took the steam out of the room before it could cloud the mirrors and soak the walls. After several minutes he was done.

Matt left the shower and had a look in the full mirror behind the sink. "Not bad, for an old guy" he said as he flexed. After shaving and looking after his ablutions he entered his walk in closet and chose some clothes. Now dressed in silk pants, a cotton short sleeved shirt and brown leather slip on shoes, no socks, he was ready for the day.

"Maria!" he called. "What's for breakfast today?"

Maria answered from the kitchen. "Eggs, sausage, hash browns, orange juice and coffee! Senor."

"Bueno! Gracias, Maria" Matt said. Good, thanks Maria.

"Ustedes agradable, Senor" you are welcome Sir, Maria called.

Matt walked into the kitchen and sat down. Picking up the morning paper he sipped his coffee and read the headlines.

"LOS GATOS WEEKLY TIMES, October 18, 2004

COMET IMPACT IMMINENT!

A comet from outer space has been detected on a collision course with Earth. Experts say that it will enter our atmosphere in less than 48 hours.

First observed from South America at the ESO Observatory, in Paranal, Chile, the comet has been named "Manheim One" or M1 after Derek Manheim the astronomer who first viewed the comet. The comet is now visible with the naked eye from dusk to dawn throughout North America. "This is a confirmed sighting" said Frederick Schoefield, Director of the observatory. "There is, however, much we don't know about the composition of the Meteorite." He stated to the media early this morning from his office at the ESO observatory. "We are running scans of the meteorite as we speak to determine its composition. The results of the scan will be forthcoming as soon as we know, you will all know." He further commented that if the comet is dense it could have catastrophic results throughout the West Coast of North America from California all the way to Alaska. "I have encouraged the Authorities to evacuate coastal areas in an effort to minimize the casualties from the potential tidal waves that will occur immediately after impact in the Pacific Ocean."

He went on to say that if the comet is less dense than predicted, it will not cause quite the devastation it would if it were a denser comet. However, it will have a more widespread effect on the environment as it may break up into smaller pieces and may even hit populated areas.

As usually happens whenever a comet is predicted to hit the Earth, Doomsdayers are claiming the end of the World. A group out of San Francisco called the Servants of God is holding vigils at Long Beach proclaiming repentance and salvation to those who turn to God now. "Now is the time to get right with God! The end is near! Don't hesitate you will meet God soon, prepare yourselves!" Pastor Don Sellars suggests. He goes on to say that when the end comes, many will wait too long to cry out to God and be lost. Skeptics say that the Earth will be just fine and the comet will pass by just like all the others.

Federal Emergency Measures Agency (FEMA) has issued evacuation notices for all cities in the western seaboard. Scott Drummond of FEMA asks all citizens to evacuate in an orderly fashion. A State of Emergency has been declared in California, Oregon and Washington States. Alaska is still considering its response. The National Guard is assisting in all effected states and has been given extreme powers to control looting. Evacuation routes are marked in yellow and traffic lights are being controlled by FEMA to regulate the evacuations.

President George Bush stated at an address to the Nation this morning from the White House that… "I want our citizens to know that we are doing all in our power to limit the potential fall out from this incredible event. I know that I can rely on our citizens to evacuate with calm and composure. America will remain strong during this terrible disaster and I know Americans can be trusted to react with dignity and courage."

Matt set the paper down. He rose from his chair and walked outside through the massive glass doors, then continued on till he stopped at the edge of his deck. Looking skyward he could see in the growing dawn a bright light just over the horizon to the north. Could that be it, he thought to himself.

Moving over to his left he focused his telescope on the northern light. Sure enough he could see a ball of light with twin tails streaming eastward. I guess it's not a hoax, he said to himself.

Walking back through the kitchen he continued through to his office. "Lights" he commanded. The office lights came on at his command. Sitting at his desk he moved his computer mouse to activate his computers Plasma screen. Flipping between programs he brought up his schedule and confirmed his appointment for this morning at 9:00 at the University of Berkley, California.

"Progress can't wait for natural disasters!" he said to himself, "better get moving." Matt gathered his laptop, his vacuum sealed tube of nanobots, and his research papers and headed for the door.

"Maria, I'm off to the university. Back by noon." He called.

"Bueno, Senor!" Maria said as she cleaned up the wasted breakfast.

His Chrysler Crossfire was parked out front and he leapt in with the agility his training provided. The Crossfire Convertible had a supercharged 330 horse power engine with over 300 pounds of torque which gave the nimble machine excellent acceleration that competed with many more expensive European sports cars.

With the top open Matt drove down his long driveway and through the iron gates that opened automatically. He put the car through its paces as he negotiated the curves of Alma Bridge Road and down on to the Santa Cruz Highway.

He arrived in record time at Berkley, parked and jumped out setting the alarm on from his key fob. A state of the art security system on the Crossfire disabled the ignition system, set the security alarm and beeped in reply.

Matt entered the lecture hall with his wares and greeted the security guard by name. The hall was filled to capacity. "Better than I expected Manuel!" he called as he set up on the stage. "Si Senor, mucho bueno" Manuel replied with enthusiasm.

The assembled guests included doctors, scientists, students and faculty. Members of the press were ready with their recorders and notepads.

Also present were pharmaceutical company representatives with large frowns on their faces. Obviously upset by the potential success of this public experiment they could stand to lose millions in revenue if the nanobot technology proved successful.

Rebecca Forster arrived and was wheeled by a nurse to the center stage. "Hi Rebecca, are you ready to change the world?" Matt asked enthusiastically.

"You bet Matt, I can't wait!" Rebecca replied eagerly.

Rebecca Forster was a terminal cancer patient. Cancer had done its best to kill Rebecca since she was diagnosed 18 months ago. The cancer had started in her left breast and had spread to her lymph nodes and lungs in rapid succession. Several bouts of chemotherapy had done nothing to slow its progress and only left her weaker. She had weeks to live at best and was eager to try this new treatment.

Matt helped Rebecca onto the bed at centre stage with the help of Dr. Francis Magee and Nurse Rose Fuentes who were both on staff at the university.

Dr. Magee was the head of the Medical Department at Berkley. At six foot tall, one 150 pounds. His thinning red hair and ruddy complexion gave him the look of a kindly professor, helped by the bow tie he always wore under his doctor's whites.

Nurse Fuentes was a short round woman who looked like she could both cook and eat well. She was an experienced nurse who had been at the University looking after the needs of the students for many years. She was compassionate and liked by everyone she met.

"We'll get you hooked up now, Rebecca. We'll proceed in a few moments." said Matt. "Don't worry, everything will be just fine."

"Okay." Rebecca said with a nervous sigh.

Matt proceeded to the podium, booted up his laptop and interfaced wirelessly with the equipment hidden behind the curtain at the back of the stage. The screen behind him came to life as he started his presentation. A computer generated video began showing the nanobots being injected into a human body, and hunting down cancer cells.

"Honored guests; Doctors; ladies and gentlemen! Thank you for coming today. My name is Matthew Parker and you are about to witness an historical event! Never before have we seen the science of medicine and technology merge to this extent to benefit mankind. The ability to build micro machines capable of seeking out and destroying cancer cells, while at the same time triggering cellular regeneration, is unheard of. Today, we do have the knowledge we have been lacking. The nanobots I have created, will revolutionize medicine as we know it. Not only can they rid the body of cancer cells, they can be programmed to identify and destroy any harmful cells from the entire human body."

The microscopic spider like creatures moved in for the kill cutting out one cell at a time and ripping it to pieces. Antibodies now saw what was left of the cancer cells and attacked them as foreign objects. The nanobots then punctured a healthy cell and a small arc of electricity was seen as the cell was stimulated to reproduce. It soon split into two, then three as the audience watched. The nanobots were removed and the video ended.

Matt continued, "Rebecca Forster has volunteered to undergo the first human test of this procedure. We will be injecting her with nanobots that have been programmed to eliminate the cancer cells from her body. At the same time the nanobots will stimulate the healthy cells to regenerate the damaged tissue. Her lymph nodes, mammary glands and lungs will within hours, be as good as new. Within days she will be completely healthy with no trace of cancer anywhere!"

Polite applause came from the audience. One reporter asked, "Mr. Parker, you are not a doctor, how is it that you are allowed to practice medicine?"

"I am not a doctor, but a research scientist and physicist. I developed the technology to create the nanobots using carbon molecules. The nanobots can be directed to create duplicates of themselves, just like a human cell reproduces, the nanobots can construct new machines if provided the raw material. Once I saw the potential benefits to the medical field, I consulted with my friend Dr Magee here," he waved his hand at the doctor, "to conduct experiments, get FDA approval for human testing and finally execute the test here."

"Have you not tested in a human subject before? If not, isn't it risky to conduct this experiment with the world watching?" asked the same reporter.

"Not at all, I am supremely confident in the results of this demonstration. Thousands of hours of testing in lab animals have been successful. I have no reason to doubt that we will also be successful here today." Answered Matt.

"What are the risks to Miss Forster?" another reporter asked.

"Dr. Magee, would you like to answer this question?" asked Matt.

"Certainly Matthew" Dr. Magee continued, "The risks are at best, minimal. Rebecca may experience some discomfort as the nanobots are injected, and then again when they start to destroy the cancer cells. Nurse Fuentes and I will be watching her closely and providing any medication as necessary. Emergency services are on standby and can be here in minutes if needed."

"If there are no further questions, I think it's time to begin." said Matt.

Matt walked over to Rebecca and asked, "You OK?"

"Yes, please go ahead." Rebecca answered.

"Alright. Doctor, are you ready?"

"All set!" Dr. Magee responded.

"Nurse Fuentes?"

"Ready"

Matt picked up the tube of nanobots and said to the audience "This contains the nanobots that we will inject into Rebecca through a hypodermic needle. Over five thousand will be injected into her body and within minutes will start their work."

He opened the tube and removed a canister of liquid containing the nanobots. He passed it to Dr. Magee who inserted an hypodermic needle and removed a full syringe of the green fluid. Vital signs were now displayed on the big screen as well as an image of Rebecca's face and a 3D diagram of her body.

"As you can see on the screen, the diagram will show the progress of the nanobots through Rebecca's body. They are carbon based machines which would be difficult to track. However, each nanobot contains a radioactive isotope which will allow the sensors to track them quite accurately. Please begin Doctor." Matt began

Dr. Magee approached Rebecca, lifted her arm, placed a tourniquet at her biceps and found the vein. He then proceeded to inject the fluid into her arm. Rebecca winced slightly as the fluid was injected.

"Rebecca will feel a slight burning sensation as the nanobots are injected but it will pass. As you can see on the screen the mass of nanobots have entered her system and will be distributed through her blood stream."

On the screen a mass of green glowing dots began disbursing through her arm and up towards her heart, stopping there and then spreading throughout her body. Within minutes the nanobots could be seen everywhere her arteries and veins allowed. Soon they could be seen congregating at the cancer sites in her lymph nodes, breasts and lungs.

"The nanobots have detected the cancer cells and will immediately begin their work." Matt commented.

As the audience watched Rebecca squirmed uncomfortably. Dr. Magee had earlier connected a Saline drip and now added a mild sedative and low grade pain killer to the IV line. Rebecca soon calmed down and was resting comfortably as the nanobots continued to destroy the insidious growths. A new mass of green dots glowed in the center of the diagram of Rebecca's body.

"As you can see another mass was found near Rebecca's spinal column. This was previously undetected by MRI scans. The nanobots will find and eradicate any cancer cells in Rebecca." Matt continued.

The nanobots could be seen coursing again through her blood stream. They were still actively seeking out any further cancer cells but all had been obliterated.

"I will now ask Doctor Magee to insert a hypodermic into Rebecca's arm with several cancer cells in it. The nanobots will find them in a few minutes and can be easily removed, along with the cells."

Dr. Magee started to insert the needle when Rebecca suddenly groaned and went into spasms. Her vital signs went crazy and were visible on the view screen. The crowd gasped as Matt shouted "What's going on Doctor?"

"I don't know why, but she's entered cardiac arrest!" Dr. Magee responded as he jumped into action. There was a flurry of activity as they tried to stabilize Rebecca. "Matthew, call an ambulance!"

Matthew pressed the emergency button on the podium and the Emergency Crew was on its way.

"Is she going to be OK?" Matt asked

"I'm doing everything I can!" Dr. Magee answered "I just don't know what happened!"

Suddenly a solid line appeared on the monitors and a long audible beep was heard.

"I've lost her!" Dr. Magee exclaimed.

"Do something, there is no explanation for this!" Matt shouted

"I've done everything I can!" shouted the doctor in response

Matt walked to the podium. "Ladies and gentlemen. I'm sorry, but I'll have to ask you to leave. Obviously, this didn't go exactly as planned. Emergency Paramedics should be here any minute and they'll need room to work. Please exit by the rear doors in an orderly fashion."

The audience rose as one and left murmuring indistinctly to themselves. Except one reporter. "This definitely will make the front page. History in the making! Death by technology!" he shouted as he left.

One man remained and stood quietly in the shadows unnoticed as the paramedics arrived and rushed to the stage. He was dressed in a white summer suit, covered with a tan trench coat and on his head sat a white panama hat. His black curly hair was visible over his ears and over his collar but his long sideburns showed flecks of grey. An unlit cigar was in his mouth, as was always the case for him. He had the build of a wrestler that had not wrestled for years, but there was no mistaking the power in his frame.

The paramedics left with the covered body of Rebecca Forster on a gurney as Matt Parker sat despondent on the stage, head in hands. "I'm sorry Rebecca" he sighed.

Doctor Magee spoke silently with Nurse Fuentes for a few moments then she headed off stage. He waked over to Matt put a hand on his shoulder and said "We'll find out what happened Matthew, I promise you!" Then he walked towards the exit.

As he approached the rear of the room he heard a voice whisper to him, "Doctor!" He saw the man in the shadows, looked quickly back at Matt then joined the mysterious man in the darkness. "Not here!" the Doctor said vehemently. "It's too dangerous!"

"Relax *Doctor*; no one is around to see us here. Your payment for a job well done!" the man said as he handed the Doctor a thick brown envelope. Doctor Magee quickly hid the envelope in his jacket. "I'm sure you will find it will more than compensate you for two minutes work."

"$1,500,000 in stock options in Gerald Pharmaceuticals? I would think so. Thank you." said the doctor.

"And Doctor?" asked the man.

"Yes?"

"If word gets out, your career will be finished. You need not be concerned, however. You won't live long enough to worry!" the man stated.

"Of course, Jennings, I know that. You don't have to worry about me"

"I know, Doctor. I know."

The man left by the rear door, the Doctor soon after.

Manuel stepped into the light. "Madre de Dios!" he said as he ran up to Matt. "Senor! Senor Parker!"

"What is it Manuel?" asked Matt

"I don't know how to say it. Um, the Doctor, he, he killed the lady!" Manuel said urgently.

"What do you mean? He killed Rebecca? It was my fault Manuel!"

"No, Senor. The Doctor he took money from a man named Jennings. He work for a drug company, uh, Heraldo Company."

"How do you know this Manuel?"

"I saw it. I hear it. In the back of this room. In the dark. I was watching, see. The Doctor met with the man in the shadows. They couldn't see me! I was in shadows too. What are you going to do Senor?" Manuel asked.

"I don't know. Leave it to me Manuel. Keep this between you and me for now. Don't tell anyone!" Matt ordered.

"Si Senor. Comprende. Manuel understand!" Manuel replied.

Chapter 7

Albert Jennings left the lecture hall inconspicuously and lit his cigar again with a matchstick that he struck against his heel. He savored the flavor as he puffed the stogie to life sending clouds of smoke into the air. Flicking the match away, he walked toward his car, a white 1970 Cadillac Deville. He had owned it since new and it 'fit' him he said. It was in mint condition and he had kept it that way ever since. Albert had few luxuries in his life. He had travelled the world, lived the high life when he could, but his favorite activity was intimidation. He lived in a simple apartment in New York City with a view of the statue of Liberty but barely got back there as his job kept him so busy.

Albert had never forgotten his roots. His mother and father met at Ellis Island after the Second World War. They were attracted to each other immediately. She was blond and blue eyed and thin and fragile like a beautiful flower. He was dark skinned and muscular with the looks of a Greek God.

His father, coincidentally, was Greek, giving Albert the powerful body and dark curly hair that he kept under his hat most of the time. Before the war, his father was a fisherman from a long line of fishermen, and proud of it. During the war he fought for the Greek Resistance until its end but left his home because of the continuing battle between leftist guerillas and the conservative Greek government. Peace would be a long time coming and America offered hope.

From his mother Albert inherited intelligence. She was a Russian professor of Physics at Moscow State University. They were together for several years, enough to bear one child, Albert Jennings, born Alianis Gianopoulos. Albert Jennings was just one of his many aliases. The year after Albert was born, his mother died from cancer, probably for her work with nuclear research at the university while Moscow was becoming a nuclear power under direction of Andrei Sakharov.

Albert's Father never got over her death. He took to drinking heavily and became explosively violent. He became an enforcer for the Italian mob led by Carlo Gambino in New York and soon his son followed suit as a soldier for the Mafia. Albert learned everything he knew about torture, intimidation and violence from his father.

After a few years Albert 'retired' from the mob and became an enforcer for Gerald Pharmaceuticals, a global company with divisions in everything from baby food to cancer drugs. Abvil and Zormax were household names but only a few knew the length that the company would go to get its products approved and used in the USA market, the biggest consumer of prescription drugs in the world.

A 1998 study showed that Americans consumed 15 tons of aspirin per day and 19 billion tablets per year. Big "pharma" spends $11 billion per year on marketing and Gerald Pharmaceuticals was leading the pack in record profits.

Albert Jennings knew what went on behind the scenes; bribery, intimidation, 'accidental deaths', arson, even murder if necessary. He had a good record with Gerald. The 'law' had never been able to trace anything back to him or the company. He had learned his trade well.

His bribery and intimidation of Dr. Francis Magee was not even considered work by Albert. In fact, he was enjoying seeing him squirm. He would have done it for free, but if he did, he would ruin his reputation.

Albert got into his Cadillac and started the big car. He smiled again as the engine purred quietly. He eased it from the curb and pulled away, classical music poured from his windows. He had to get to the safe house and relax for a while. He had a suspicion that Dr. Francis Magee or Matthew Parker might give him some trouble. He smiled even wider and blew smoke out the window as he drove away thinking of how he could creatively persuade them to tow the company line.

Chapter 8

Melinda Chase sat at a small table in her kitchen nook and sipped her morning coffee. She looked out the window as she listened to the radio tuned to the All News and Talk radio station. Golfers already on their second round were visible in the distance on the Druid Hills Golf course. With a crisp but sunny and beautiful day ahead, it was a perfect day for golf. The birds sang their welcome to the day as the steam quietly disappeared from the rolling hills of the well-manicured fairways and greens. The announcer interrupted her peace and quiet with a news bulletin.

"Today, the world watches and waits. Within minutes Manheim One, the Meteor from Saturn, is scheduled to impact in the Pacific Ocean. Evacuations are near completion from San Francisco to Seattle and every coastal city in between. FEMA media relations director Scott Drummond said "The evacuees have been put up in shelters further in land and are cooperating with authorities. Those citizens, who have disobeyed the evacuation order and have chosen to remain in their homes, do so at their own risk and FEMA cannot be held responsible for their safety." UPN news reported today that several black looters have been shot in Seattle by National Guard troops, causing outrage from the black community. "If these people where white, they would still be alive!" said one advocate for minority groups in a shelter outside of Portland.

The tremendous scope of these evacuations has never been seen before. Credit definitely belongs to

President Bush as he quickly declared States of emergency in all West Coast States and gave sweeping powers to FEMA under the auspices of The Department of Homeland Security.

The Canadian Emergency Preparedness organization PSEPC, however did not issue evacuation orders and claim that according to their sources the meteorite poses no threat to Canadian citizens on the West Coast. This is contrary to most experts who say that the risk is too great to do nothing."

Melinda put down her coffee and strode to the wall phone. She dialed a familiar number and was not surprised to hear "Hello" in a small voice. "Hi there! This is Aunty Mel. Who is this? Jamie?" Melinda asked.

"No, this is Samantha 'anty' Mel! " said Melinda's four year old niece Samantha.

"Hi Sam! Is your Dad there?"

"Sure, I'll get him. D-a-a-a-a-d!" Samantha yelled. "Ph-o-o-o-one!"

Melinda heard a clunk as the phone was dropped and little feet ran off in the distance. Soon after the phone rustled and squeaked as it was picked up by Melinda's brother Frank.

"Hello?" Frank said

"Hi Frank, its Mel." Melinda said quickly. "How's things? Have you heard the news today?"

"Things are fine, I'm just heading out the door to work. What news?"

"Oh, just the end of the world. Don't you listen to the radio?"

"No time. I usually listen on the way to work. What do you mean the end of the world?"

"A giant meteor is about to hit the earth in the Pacific Ocean and devastate the entire West Coast! Evacuations have been ordered. I can't believe a communications expert can be so out of it!" Melinda exclaimed.

"I'm a telecommunications expert, not a broadcast media executive!   Anyway, you're kidding about the Meteor, right?"

"No, I'm not. Anyway, I figured you'd be involved because the Emergency Communications Network will probably be activated if it hasn't been already."

"Well, my pager hasn't…" Frank's pager went off as he spoke. "…*has* just gone off, so I suppose you are right!"

"OK, I'll let you go. Everything OK in Hartford?"

"Yeah, we probably won't have many problems on the East Coast anyway. The ECN should be able to handle all the emergency traffic FEMA and the National Guard will create, but I imagine that the regular telephone lines must be going crazy as relatives try to reach evacuees in the West. I better get to work. Thanks for your call Mel."

"You're welcome Frank. Take care of all those kids, huh."

"I keep telling you Mel, only six!"

"Only! Love ya!"

"Love ya!, bye."

"Bye."

Melinda hung up the phone, walked back to the table, downed her coffee and headed for her bedroom. After dressing in a sky blue silk suit, with a sheer white blouse and matching shoes, Melinda picked up her briefcase, her cell phone and her color coordinated leather purse. She headed for the front entrance and left through the beautiful rich mahogany double doors. Crossing the veranda and down the stairs Melinda looked back just before she opened her car door. Set back from the road and surrounded by ancient dogwood trees the house looked like something out of Gone With The Wind.

The house was built in 1890 after the civil war and Melinda spent thousands of dollars to bring it up to today's standards while keeping the character of the old place. She bought the house from an old southern belle who lost her husband a couple of years ago and found the house too much to keep up. She couldn't afford extra help, so with the sale of the home, moved into a senior's complex that still allowed her her freedom, but didn't require her assistance to keep the place clean. She was soon in her element as the prettiest 84 year old in the place. Several elderly gentlemen were fighting for her attention the last time Melinda visited her.

Melinda got into her car, a black Jeep Cherokee provided by CDC and drove out her azalea lined drive way. As she rolled onto Lullwater drive her mind turned to work. She picked up her cell phone and called into the office.

After only one ring Charlotte answered "CDC, Ms. La Roche speaking. How may I be of assistance?"

"It's me, Char. Is the team in yet?" asked Melinda

"Oh, good morning Melinda. Well, Jacob is here, and Noah, but Sam and Rhonda haven't arrived yet. They would usually be in by now."

"OK, could you page Sam for me and ask him to move it? I expect we're going to have a busy day. Did you here about the Meteorite?"

"Yes, I did. Isn't it just terrible? It must be getting close to impact by now, don't you think?"

"Well, that's why we'll be needed. I expect a call from FEMA any time to help with evaluating the fallout from the flooding on the West Coast. I need Sam and Rhonda there by the time I get there. I expect they are together so forget protocol and tell them both to get in ASAP. I'm 20 minutes away now."

"Very well, Melinda. I'll get right on it. See you soon" Charlotte said.

"Shortly, thanks Charlotte." Melinda said as she hung up and continued on her route to CDC.

Chapter 9

Derek Manheim started as the Artificial Intelligence driven computer wakened him with a feminine voice. *"Derek, scans complete, data analysis complete."*

"What? Who?" groggily he asked.

"Derek, the scans of the meteor are complete. Data analysis complete. Would you like me to summarize?" the computer asked.

"Yes, yes, of course, please go ahead KAMY. What time is it?" Derek asked.

"I am a multimillion dollar artificial intelligence system, and you want to know what time it is?" asked the computer as if offended.

"Yes KAMY, what time is it?"

"At the tone, it will be 9:45AM Tuesday October, 19ʰ 2004. B-E-E-E-E-P."

"Very funny, KAMY. Please summarize the analysis of the meteorite and give me a printout." Commanded Derek.

"Working...

After conducting infrared, dopler, radiation spectral photometry Etc. Analysis indicates that the Meteorite is 99.9 percent H20." KAMY reported.

"What is the other point 1 percent?"

"It could not be determined from the data available."

"You don't know?"

"It could not be determined from the data available."

"Like I said… Anyway, I knew its mass was too small for a meteorite that size but water? It will break up before it can reach the lower atmosphere." Derek stated.

"Correct, Derek. My analysis predicts that as the Meteor approaches the Earth, it will increase in speed exponentially until it cannot possibly hold together and will break up into approximately eight smaller pieces. Each of those will launch on its own trajectory and enter the Earth's atmosphere at different locations on the globe. However, no impacts will occur because the smaller pieces will burn up in the atmosphere. None will reach the surface of the earth." KAMY concluded.

"I agree with your analysis KAMY. Good work!" said Derek as if to a coworker.

"Thank you Derek. Will there be anything else?"

"Yes, KAMY, please continue recording the meteorites trajectory. When will the meteorite enter the atmosphere?"

"The meteorites will enter the atmosphere in twenty two minutes."

"Thanks, KAMY, that's all for now."

"You are welcome Derek."

Derek touched his earpiece. "Call Frederick Schofield." After a moment he heard Frederick answer. *"Yes, Derek, what is it? I am about to speak to the press."*

"Sorry to interrupt Frederick, but I have some good news about the meteorite!"

"Good news, what good news?"

"KAMY has finished the scans of the meteorite and we don't have anything to worry about. It is made up almost entirely of water. It will break up in the atmosphere and there will be no impacts at all!" Derek exclaimed joyfully.

"You can't be serious! I will be the laughing stock of the scientific community if this gets out. Don't you realize that upon my recommendation they have evacuated millions of people around the world from coastal areas at an innumerable financial and political cost? It could ruin my reputation, not to mention your career, Derek." Frederick blustered.

"What are you saying? That we keep quiet about this? You must be crazy, this is great news! People can go home without fear!"

"And if you're wrong Derek? What then? In twenty minutes it will be all over either way and it will make no difference. We'll keep this between you and me for now. Yes?"

"I guess." Derek sighed. "I guess that makes sense, in a bizarre kind of way. Alright, have it your way doc." Derek capitulated.

"You won't regret this Derek, I assure you. Yes, yes, people I'm coming. I have to go, my press awaits me! Frederick out." Frederick said as he hung up.

Derek slouched in his chair. He didn't feel right about holding back this important information, but there wasn't anything he could do about it either. So he swiveled his chair around and watched Manheim One on the wall screen until the meteorite broke up into eight pieces and disintegrated in the atmosphere in a fiery display.

Chapter 10

Branford Harbor is blessed with a long shoreline which includes the beaches at: Short Beach, Double Beach, Indian Neck, Limewood Beach, Hotchkiss Grove, Pine Orchard, and Stoney Creek. It lies at the entrance of the Branford River with Johnson Point on the West and Jeffrey Point on the East.

Frank Chase left his home in Branford Harbor and headed for CTTEL in New Haven, Connecticut. He took Short Beach road to Route 1, then onto State Highway 95 to 91 and into town. He reached The Connecticut Telcom building on Chapel Street, parked and stepped out of his BMW 330Ci convertible. At 230 horsepower and with European handling, the BMW was a fun ride. His commute seemed shorter, even though he occasionally got caught in traffic as he got closer to New Haven.

The sports car was a reward to himself for completing his Masters in Electrical Engineering at MIT eighteen months ago. The leave of absence he took from work allowed him to complete his graduate studies in record time while allowing him to hold on to his job. Of course, he couldn't be replaced, according to his boss, Mike Swaronski, who would basically pay Frank whatever he wanted to keep him at CTTEL.

Frank's pager went off again. "I'm coming!" he said to the device on his belt as he turned it off. He climbed the steps of the concrete and glass building, passed through security and took the stairs to the basement. There he placed his ID card against the card reader beside the door and entered the Network Operations Center or NOC (like knock) as everyone called it.

Once inside he passed through a pressure door that allowed the NOC to remain free of outside air contaminants, and maintain an air conditioned, temperature controlled environment. It was almost as secure as a biological hazard containment system not unlike that in a Biotech company, although not as efficient. The biggest difference between the two was the temperature. In order to keep the high tech computer equipment cool, the inside thermostat was kept at a cool 58 degrees Fahrenheit.

The NOC held millions of dollars of network switches, computer storage, imaging and recording devices. It was the central hub through which all of Connecticut's communication channels flowed. This included internet, telephone, data, cellular, whether it was across fiber optics, through the air, or across copper wire, it passed through this central hub. If Connecticut failed, it would affect New York, New Jersey, Massachusetts and the rest of the east coast, from Washington in the south to Montreal in Canada in the North.

Frank Chase was the glue that held it all together. He was the NOC Senior Operator and Engineer. He was responsible for the dozen men and women that maintained and monitored the sophisticated equipment that made up the central hub. Three shifts covered the equipment twenty four hours a day, seven days a week. Redundant systems permitted the close knit group to have the networks up and running with absolutely no down time. Fail-safes were in place that made it almost impossible to overload a channel through the network. However, the network traffic created by the Manheim One incident on the West Coast had brought many routes from the west through the hub into the danger zone. A few more percent and a channel could crash and burn. Then a cascading effect could occur which would in turn bring down channel after channel until the entire hub could be brought down. This would result in the entire Eastern Seaboard being without communications.

Frank walked through the maze of humming and beeping equipment to the core of the facility. It housed a control console in a C shaped arrangement that had several control buttons, read outs and blinking lights. Frank sat in the center of the C like a starship Captain. In front of him was a wall sized view screen with a variable display upon which Frank could call up diagnostics, network diagrams, flow control, and even individual network streams. The screen was currently displaying a network diagram of all flows through the hub. Each type of traffic was highlighted a different color which varied depending on its bandwidth and remaining capacity. As was typical green was good, yellow was worth watching, orange was marginal, and red was bad.

Frank was looking at the view screen in astonishment as the spider's web of network routes was indicating a lot of orange and several red flows, primarily in voice communication. "I thought so!" said Frank to no one in particular.

He worked the keyboard and console in front of him like a concert pianist until, one by one, the reds changed to orange. He categorized the types of flows from critical to minor in importance and then prioritized them. The Emergency Communications Network, or ECN, being the highest priority. Frank was redirecting a percentage of the flows from several of the blocked channels to ones more able to handle extra traffic. After a few more minutes many of the oranges changed to yellow, and yellows to green.

After 45 minutes Frank sat back, exhaled, and relaxed in his ergonomic chair. Another crisis averted he thought to himself.

Frank rose from his chair, took another glance at the view screen and walked satisfied from the core. He went over to the staff coffee area and poured himself a coffee. Joan Nygard walked up as well. "Hi Frank. Everything OK now?" she asked with a knowing smile on her face.

"Yup. I took care of it. How are the systems holding up?" Frank asked acknowledging her smile with one of his own.

"No problem. Everything's cool!" she responded. "Accept that you were going to show me how to recalibrate the motherboard on the SX-10 multiplexer. Remember?"

"Oh yeah, I forgot about that." Frank said as he smirked into his coffee.

"Yeah right, you have been avoiding it for days now! Do you have the time now *Mr*. Chase? Please?"

"OK. Let's finish our coffees and head over to the shop." Frank said raising his hands in the air in surrender.

They spoke for a few minutes about work, kids, and upcoming vacations. Frank liked Joan. She had a fast intelligence and dry sense of humor made her especially fun to be around. They had a good friendship both inside and outside of work.

Joan and her husband often brought their kids over to Franks to spend the weekend. They would go boating and swimming and have barbeques on the beach together. Joan's three kids got along well with Frank's six and often the day ended with a ball game and ice cream. Days of laughter and fun would be treasured memories for both families.

At work Joan was an effective systems trouble shooter. She could diagnose system errors and read event logs faster than anyone Frank knew. She had worked her way up in CTTEL from an administration clerk to Systems Maintenance Engineer over the last ten years by spending every spare moment studying and asking questions of those more experienced than her. She was a quick study and Frank didn't mind spending time adding to her skills.

Frank and Joan walked over to the east side of the NOC where the work shop was located so it could make use of external venting. Joan pulled out a circuit board from among many on a shelf in a cabinet marked spares and set it on the desk. "This is a motherboard from the SX-10." She said. "I replaced it with a new one last week. This one was causing faults in the system and when I traced the faults in the logs, it said the board was out of calibration. So, where do we start?"

"Well, first we need to hook it up to the computer to recreate the faults. Then we have to trace the faults to the troublesome chip. Once that is identified we can run some test programs on the chip to determine where the problem is. All we have to do after that is run the calibration program and tweak the chip to spec. That's it!"

Joan let out a slow whistle, "Is that all! You make it sound so easy."

"It is! Once you've done two or three of them you'll be a pro." Frank responded. "Let's get started." Frank took the circuit board from Joan and attached it to the computer by the interface cable. For the next hour and one half they worked together until it was done.

"That wasn't too bad. I think I can handle it. Of course you are a good teacher."

"You are a quick study Joan. I'm impressed with your grasp of the process. You do the next one while I watch and then you'll be on your own. I better get back to the core and see what's going on. See you later." said Frank as he left.

"Thanks again Frank. See ya!" Joan stored the repaired mother board in the spares cabinet and went back to work. Joan liked Frank watched him leave with a smile.

At six foot two and two hundred and forty pounds, he was a little on the heavy side, a result of pumping iron and playing football in college. He had black hair, parted to one side, with a little grey forming on his temples. The sun had taken its toll on his face over the years and the crow's feet around his eyes gave others the impression that he was always smiling. He kept a tan all year even though the Connecticut sun didn't always appear in the winter, but boating on the wind swept shore of Branford Harbor always gave his face some color.

Frank took another look at the board and with a couple of minor adjustments to the flow everything was looking good. Frank picked up the phone and called Atlanta. When the ringing stopped Melinda's voice said *"CDC Melinda Chase."*

"Hi Mel, it's Frank."

"Hey Frank. What's up?" Melinda asked.

"What's happening with the Meteor?" Frank asked quickly.

"Nothing. It burned up in the atmosphere. No impact. No tidal waves. The media is saying that if it wasn't for the actual sighting, it was a non-event. People are moving home and of course, many are complaining that they moved for nothing."

"Typical! People are never satisfied, are they? The evacuations could have saved their life. Just because the unexpected happened, they complain about the inconvenience. They would be singing a different tune if the meteor actually impacted wouldn't they?"

"You bet! Well, I guess life will go back to normal now that the danger is passed. How was the communications network affected?"

"It was touch and go for a while, but I got it back in line in about an hour. Thanks again for the heads up."

"No problem. I should get back to work. Iraq will be the hotspot now. The terrorists released a biological weapon in the south to push the Americans out. It backfired on them and thousands of Iraqis are dead. It is terrible. We're still evaluating the situation. We haven't heard from the State Department yet, but I bet you can imagine what his response will be."

"I can imagine it will be quick and effective." Frank commented dryly.

"Uh-huh. Anyhow, give my love to Maureen and the kids."

"Will do. How's Jessica? "

"She is rebellious, incommunicative, and stubborn. The same as ever."

"You need to give her some love, Mel. It's all about insecurity since the divorce. She needs to know that you love her and accept who she is."

"I know that Frank. It's just hard. She's so much like me at that age. I sometimes wonder what I put Mom through!"

"From what I remember, quite a bit. My little sister spent more time grounded then not. But you grew out of it, and so will she. Just give her some time, AND attention."

"I'll try! Thanks Frank. Got to go."

"OK Mel, take care."

"Bye, Frank."

Frank set down the phone and got back to monitoring the network. There were still a few yellow zones but nothing too serious. It was probably a result of all the refugees phoning relatives and FEMA and the National Guard coordinating the return of the citizens to their cities.

Chapter 11

Point one percent. Point one percent doesn't sound like much. How could such an insignificant figure have the potential to change mankind forever?

When M1 broke up in the upper atmosphere it broke into eight pieces. Each of those eight pieces burned up in the atmosphere as the hardened, ancient ice that made up most of the meteorites melted. This left only the point one percent of matter contained in the ice. This unknown matter, if it was any kind of metal or rock, would have been destroyed in the heat created by reentry. Impervious to heat, but not to pressure, this matter broke down into microscopic particles while the meteorites plummeted through the layers of atmosphere until it reached the troposphere where it was captured by the clouds and carried like dust in various directions by the winds of the world.

One weather system moved quickly in from the east blasting the coast of India with more rain. It pelted down onto the province of Karaikal, exacerbating the flooding already there. The Manheim particles were carried in by the clouds and dropped with the rain to join the water already there. Just one more contaminant added to the already noxious mix of sewage, mud and chemicals from the farms, homes, and factories overwhelmed by the monsoons.

Water was neck deep in the town of Karaikal. The rivers and waterways usually pure and blue were brown and muddy as the run off carried mud and debris into it.

One small 8 year old boy struggled against the current that pushed him along the way far, far from his home. He called out to anyone to help him, but others within sight were struggling for survival as well.

A small boat carrying two men in fluorescent vests and hard hats fought against the current, looking for survivors of the flooding. As they motored along they heard the child's voice and looked around them. One saw his hand waving to them through the wind and rain, then pointed and shouted. The boat turned in the direction he had indicated and struggled across the current to rescue the child. The small boy went under, once, twice, and was gone from view.

Only the water could be seen for a while and then he surfaced again, sputtering, brown water from his nose and mouth. With a quick turn the boat was upon him. The tall man who steered the boat, reached down into the water with a gaff and pulled up the boy by his shirt. The other man, the shorter one, grabbed onto the boy with his hands and pulled him into the boat. The boy had stopped breathing.

Quickly the short man started CPR. His first aid training as a fire warden at a local factory came in handy. He raised the boy's neck, opened his airway and applied his lips to the boy's to make an airtight seal. Blowing into the boy's mouth, he shared life giving oxygen. After a few minutes the boy coughed and water exploded from his mouth, just as the man was about to blow in again. The water was forced into the mouth of the short man, and into his sinuses and out his nose. The man coughed himself, and blew his nose with his thumb and cursed to himself, but he was pleased that the boy was alive and hugged him to his chest to warm the boy. He wrapped the boy in a blanket and looked for more survivors.

This one Manheim particle was warm and moist again. Like a seed that needs water to germinate, the particle came to life. Root-like fingers spread out from the molecule and attached to the soft tissue in the boy's lungs. Once attached, it started to grow in size. Within minutes the molecule had become a living organism. This life form, like a virus, replicated and spread throughout the boy's bloodstream. Invading new organs and rooting quietly, unnoticed by the boy, but not for long. The boy soon started to sweat as his temperature rose quickly. He started to shake and cough raggedly as if he had the flu. With a sneeze the alien virus was transferred to the tall man steering the boat.

The boat was found two days later, caught in the branches of a fallen tree. Rescue workers carefully removed three bodies from the boat wondering what happened.

It looked as if there was blood coming from the mouths of the dead, but the blood was foamy and the victim's tongues were swollen and protruding. They added them to the other bodies found floating in the water. There seemed to be too many this monsoon season.

A light rain continued to fall, getting into the eyes and mouth of those seeking to rescue victims of the flood. The Manheim virus had found a new host. Man.

Chapter 12

Jacob Wettstien hung up the phone at CDC headquarters in Atlanta. His desk was a mess. Papers, notes and file folders littered the surface and his credenza was overflowing with stacks of magazines, periodicals and volumes of medical journals. Jacob put down his pencil, removed his reading glasses and rubbed his eyes. He had just been talking to his contact General Johnny "Red" Callaghan at the State Department.

The President had authorized a retaliatory attack against Al Qaeda terrorist encampments in Northern Iraq using tactical nuclear weapons. Red had told him it was going to happen within 24 hours and to watch the media.

Jacob was horrified. The attack was overkill as far as he was concerned, but he understood how the American public would accept it as a necessary response to the biological weapons released against its troops.

However, all Jacob could see was the very real civilian casualties from the fallout of the nuclear devices. In his mind's eye he could see the faces of Iraqis melting off as the radiation burns ate away their flesh. He could hear the screams of children as they wondered why they were in such pain. He could hear the cries of outrage from the Iraqis men as they held their AK47s in the air. He could hear the haunting, lilting cries from the men and women as they grieved the loss of their loved ones.

Jacob sighed as he arose from his desk and walked over to the water cooler to ease his suddenly dry throat.

Melinda Chase breezed in and waved a "Hello" on her way to her office. Jacob waved in response and followed her in.

"Hey Jacob, you look like you just lost your best friend. What's up?" Melinda asked.

"I just spoke with Red Callaghan. The President is going to retaliate with a tactical strike on Al Qaeda strong holds using nuclear weapons." Jacob said with sadness.

"Isn't that a little extreme? The civilian casualties will just add to the mayhem in the already chaotic country." Melinda exclaimed.

"Exactly, but there is nothing I could say to Red that would change his mind. The President's mind is fixed on teaching the Iraqis that biological weapons will not be tolerated."

"Does Red know where the biological weapons came from?"

"Not exactly, but Saddam threatened to use them against Israel a few years ago and it was Bush's justification for attacking Iraq in the first place. One can only assume that the weapons inspectors missed a cache stored in those caves somewhere in the mountains."

"Well, let's deal with one thing at a time. We need to know what was in those biological weapons so that we can begin to treat any survivors. There will be residuals from the weapon that could still be harmful in the ground water and on the victims. With biologicals you never know what the long term effects will be. When Sam and Rhonda get in lets meet and figure out a plan of attack." Melinda concluded.

"OK. I'll be back for the meeting. I want to see what else I can find out in the meantime." Jacob said and returned to his desk.

Melinda sat behind her desk and pulled up a map of Iraq on her computer. The biological weapons had been released in As Samawah in the south west, Ad Nisiriyah in south central Iraq and Al Basrah in the south east. The yields of the weapons were such that the invisible cloud of death would spread out approximately one hundred miles in each direction.

The populace of the cities would be overcome and the outlying areas, though sparsely populated, would be severely affected as well. With a biological weapon of this type the winds would carry the disease where ever it went. There was no way to tell the life span of the organism until a sample could be analyzed.

Sam and Rhonda arrived together. Sam placed his hand on the scanner and a buzz allowed him entry. Rhonda rushed through the door with him. A klaxon sounded and red rotating lights illuminated the office in a phsycadellic display. A security team of four men and one woman arrived carrying Heckler and Koch MP5 submachine guns at the ready. Rhonda and Sam held out their ID cards like shields at arm's length as if they would ward off the security team.

"Whoa! Hang on there guys!" Sam yelled.

"On the floor! Now!" Yelled the leader of the security team.

"Wait!" shouted Rhonda.

"Now!" the leader yelled again as he lowered his weapon and forcibly pushed Sam to the ground.

Rhonda seeing his determination fell to the floor face down and said "We work here!"

"We'll see about that." said the leader as he took their ID Cards.

"Alpha One to base, ID check, Sam Smith and Rhonda Lewis."

"Dickson to Alpha One, wait one."

"Roger, base."

"Alpha One, identities confirmed. ID numbers 534569 and 445678."

"Checking... confirmed base. Reset alarm." Then he said to Sam and Rhonda. "Sorry folks. Can't be too careful you know. Next time, enter one at a time and we won't have this problem."

Sam and Rhonda rose slowly to their feet. Rhonda started, "I know that, it's just that we were in a hurry and..."

Melinda arrived on the scene and asked, "Everyone OK? What's going on?"

"These two forgot procedure and tried to enter the wing together." The security team leader said.

"We were trying to get here as quick as we could…" Sam began.

"…and I forgot to swipe my card!" Rhonda finished.

"OK. I'll vouch for these two Mac." Melinda said to the team leader John McKenzie.

"It's alright Ms. Chase, they checked out. We'll be on our way." Mac said to Melinda, then to his team. "Let's go!"

The security team left as one in military fashion. Melinda, Sam and Rhonda headed for Melinda's office.

Noah came out of the washroom looking concerned. "What's going on?" he asked as he walked into Melinda's office and sat down.

"Nothing, it was just Sam and Rhonda checking out our security system." Commented Jacob with a smirk as entered the office and sat down.

Sam rolled his eyes and Rhonda blushed. The two took their seats at the table and tried to look as if nothing had happened.

Charlotte came in with a tray of coffee and set it on the table at one end. "Help yourselves!" she said then sat down herself and opened her laptop which was already in place at her seat. The team each took a coffee, doctored it and got down to business.

"I appreciate everyone getting here so quickly, despite the light show Sam and Rhonda announced their arrival with" Melinda began. There was muffled laughter, and even Sam and Rhonda joined in with relief. "Our hot spot is Iraq. Sam bring up the map please."

"Sure thing!" Sam responded.

Sam used his PDA to activate the holographic display and conjured up the globe of the world and then quickly transformed it into a cube showing Iraq on all four sides. The map showed a red zone clearly defined over the three cities hit with the biological weapons. It then spread out in a circle from about one hundred miles around each city. The circles overlapped and covered most of the south east of Iraq and affected neighboring Kuwait and Iran."

"Any word on casualties yet?" asked Noah

"Sam?" Melinda deferred.

"There is still confusion on that front. The media is reporting figures in the hundreds of thousands. However, sources closer to the action (CIA) have the figures at approximately ten thousand in each city." Sam reported.

"Rhonda, what kind of spread can we anticipate, post dispersion?" Melinda asked.

"Hard to say Melinda, without a clear knowledge of what the physical properties of the biological agent are, I would just be guessing."

"Noah, find out from your friends at the CBRNIAC if they can send us an analysis or a sample of the agent." Melinda ordered. CBRNIAC was the Chemical, Biological, Radiological and Nuclear Defense Information Analysis Center, a part of the Department of Defense.

"I'm on it" Noah said and left the room to phone his contact.

"What is the prevailing winds doing to spread the agent?"

"The winds are having no effect on the spread of the agent. It seems to have settled on the ground and is not affected by the wind. Whoever engineered it, didn't want it to spread so they made it like an insecticide that sticks where it is sprayed."

"It sounds like the work of General Ali Hassan al-Majid, Saddam Hussein's cousin. 'Chemical Ali' as he was known, is thought to have been responsible for the 1988 chemical attack on Kurds. He would have been responsible for the development of such a weapon. Information is sketchy as to his current whereabouts."

Noah returned, sat down and said "My CBRNIAC contact says they can send us the data on the chemical agent by email within a few minutes. Charlotte, can you watch my email and let us know when it arrives?"

"Sure." Charlotte replied and worked on her laptop quietly.

Melinda looked at the map and asked. "Sam, what is that orange spot growing in northern Iraq?"

"I don't know. Just a second and I'll find out." Sam played with his PDA and continued. "It looks like we've got an unknown virus at work. It sprang up in Mosul it seems pretty localized. Reports of twenty four sick and ten deceased from an unknown virus. They are having trouble identifying the source."

"We better keep an eye on that one. It seems to have an almost 50% mortality rate. Noah who has jurisdiction as far as relief or medical services that far north?" Melinda asked.

"Probably the Red Crescent, I'll see what I can find out." Noah responded, and then made a note to himself.

"Should we mobilize a team to head to Iraq to evaluate the situation? Hands on is better than hearsay." Jacob commented.

"Not yet. I want to see what we can get from CBRNIAC first. Our primary team is in Mexico City evaluating the conditions since the hurricane there. Anything yet Charlotte?" Melinda asked.

"Just checking… Yes it's here. Sam I'll send the data to you." Charlotte said.

Sam waited while the data transferred. When it was done he brought up the data on the display.

The display now showed the analysis of the biological weapon's make up. A graph showed parts per million on the left scale and chemical components on the lower scale. Spikes indicated the primary chemicals and biological agents in the toxic soup.

"Ingredients are Coumadin, Antithymocyte, Lewisite and Ebola Zaire." Sam reported.

"Jacob, what can you tell us about these ingredients?" Melinda asked

"The individual ingredients themselves are used for medicinal purposes in treating a variety of ailments. Coumadin, commonly known as warfarin, is used as a rat poison which caused a slow painful death to rodents. It is also used in mild doses in humans as an anticoagulant and blood thinner for heart attack patients and patients with blood clots. Antithymocyte globulin or ATG, is an immunosuppressive agent used in the treatment of transplant patients to mitigate rejection of donor organs. Lewisite (chlorovinyl dichloroarsine) is a blister agent primarily used to penetrate clothing and cause blistering of the skin. Noah, perhaps you would conclude with the Ebola virus." Jacob finished.

Noah explained. "The Ebola Zaire filovirus is the most lethal of the Ebola viruses with a ninety percent mortality rate. The onset of illness is abrupt and is characterized by fever, headache, joint and muscle aches, sore throat, and weakness, followed by diarrhea, vomiting, and stomach pain. A rash, red eyes, hiccups and internal and external bleeding may be seen in some patients. In combination with blood thinner, an immunosuppressive agent and with a blistering agent, this would cause tremendous pain and suffering of the victims before they died. I cannot believe man's inhumanity to man." Noah was moved to tears as he thought about the victims of this terrible attack.

Jacob went on. "In this mixture Lewisite is able to penetrate clothing and would cause skin blistering and burning everywhere on a victim's body and damage to the victims lungs and eyes. This would allow the rest of the agents to penetrate the victims system. The blood thinner and immunosuppressive drugs would enable the Ebola virus to infect the victim quickly and weaken the immune system. The viruses' effects would be one hundred times more virulent in an exposed system. Whoever the sadist was that created this biological weapon new what he was doing."

"In addition to that, the incubation period for the Ebola virus is usually 2 to 21 days. However, in combination with these drugs, it would be less than 12 hours and death would occur within 24 hours. The only good news is that Ebola doesn't have a long life outside of the body. Once it is exposed to the elements it will die within minutes. Only those immediately exposed would be affected, unless they come in contact with secretions from those still alive or from the bodies of deceased victims." Noah added.

"Horrific as it might seem, at least we know what we're dealing with. Once the US completes their attack, we'll send in a team. We need to be aware of the fallout from the nuclear devices. Jacob, did you find out anything else regarding the attack?" Melinda asked.

"No. I am sure they want to keep a lid on it until after the attack so that the surprise will be total. Red said he will let us know when it's done, but to watch the media as there will be a statement made by the President post deployment." Jacob said.

"Alright, Noah what is the treatment for Ebola Zaire?" Melinda asked.

Noah cleared his throat and steadied himself to continue. "Researchers from the Army Medical Research Institute of Infectious Diseases at Fort Detrick, Maryland have an experimental drug derived from hookworms but they said more research was needed before the drug, known as rNAPc2 for recombinant nematode anticoagulant protein c2, could become an accepted treatment for Ebola. It does, however, reduce the morality rate from 90% to 30% on victims already exposed to the virus. We may be able to get a sample from them and manufacture enough to use on the Iraqis that have contracted the disease from contact with the dead or dying. It will be too late to help anyone that was caught in the original release of the biological weapon. They will already have succumbed to it according to what we now know." Noah replied

"The World Health Organization will not allow an experimental drug to be used on humans, regardless of the consequences. We will have to be satisfied with containment." Jacob commented.

"We have the means to save countless lives with this new drug. I can't believe you would even hesitate!" Noah lamented.

"I am not hesitating! All I am saying is that we will not be allowed to use it, even if we could develop enough vaccine to be useful." Jacob said.

"That is ridiculous, we should use it anyway. These people need it to survive. If we cannot use the knowledge we have, what good are we doing here. We're a waste of space!" Noah said determinedly.

"Noah, we all feel the same way you do, but we have to work within the system. We will lose funding if we do anything illegal, and we will have to shut down and be no good to anyone. Biohazard containment is all we can do right now. We will be saving the lives of countless thousands by reducing the exposure to the people of Iraq." Melinda said calmly trying to diffuse the argument.

Rhonda interjected, "I have run a program which extrapolates the spread of Ebola in Iraq. It shows that, with no intervention, there will be approximately three hundred new deaths each day that we wait to take action. We should do something soon."

"I agree. We'll send a team on an Air Force transport first thing in the morning to coordinate the containment of the outbreak." Melinda said.

"I'll go!" said Noah eagerly.

After a brief pause, Melinda agreed. "Very well, Noah. Put a team together and get going ASAP, we'll keep you up-to-date on any new developments."

"OK, I'll put a team list together and run it by you before we deploy." Noah said as he started to rise with alacrity.

"Just wait. Let's see what else is brewing first." Melinda said raising her hand.

Noah sat down again.

Sam changed the display back to the globe and waited until everyone focused again. "The Mexico City team arrived this morning and has started setting up camp. They will issue a preliminary report by the end of the day." Sam went on. "There are also some reports coming from India that the flooding in the Karaikal province has caused more deaths than expected. There is talk that some bodies are showing signs of disease but it has yet to be confirmed. National Medical teams are dealing with it as best they can but have not found any live patients to treat. Autopsies are being performed on victims that show signs of infection, but no toxin, or virus has been identified as of yet."

There was an audible beep from the holographic display and it automatically changed to a view of the Pacific Northwest. Seattle showed an orange color surrounding the city.

"We just received an alert from the Seattle MMST. The local hospitals are being flooded with people showing symptoms of a viral infection. The Metropolitan Medical Strike Team has initiated a hot response to the incident. Hospitals are under quarantine and no one can enter or leave unless first diagnosed by Emergency medical staff. Local law enforcement has cordoned off the area around the Hospitals."

"Are there any indications as to the cause? Is it localized?" asked Jacob.

"No causes have been determined and the virus has not been identified. Hospitals affected are Virginia Mason, Childrens, Northwest, Allenmore, Harbour View, St. Joseph's and the list goes on. It seems pretty widespread." Sam reported

"Charlotte, see if you can find out who's in charge up there. This seems like more than a flu epidemic, it's happening too fast. It could be another terrorist attack." Melinda commanded.

"Just a minute…" Charlotte's fingers flew on her keyboard.

"Do we know how many cases they are dealing with?" Rhonda asked.

"Estimates at around one hundred and twenty." Sam said.

"When was the first case?" Rhonda asked again.

"First case was this morning at 6:15 am. A young 9 year old girl is in a coma and it doesn't look good." responded Sam.

Charlotte reported, "Mayor George Nicholas is in charge in Seattle, but the head of the Medical Team is Dr. Thomas Katz of the Northwest Medical Center. He also sits on the board of the King County Department of Public Health."

"See if you can get him on the phone." Melinda commanded.

Chapter 13

The rain came down in sheets as the wind carried more clouds in from the Pacific Ocean. Seattle, the rain capital of the US of A is well known for its rainfall. It may not get more rain than Miami, but it definitely gets more rainy days than anywhere else in the continental US thanks to the 'pineapple express' from Hawaii.

The jet stream brings in moisture off the Pacific Ocean and dumps it in the Pacific Northwest as the clouds get heavy and park on the North Cascade Range. Seattle, the home of the Mariners, Starbucks and the space needle is known for its laid back, coffee drinking population.

Today was a bit different for Dr. Thomas Katz as he strode through the emergency ward of the Northwest Medical Center. Normally quiet at this time of day, the corridors were filled with patients on gurneys. Dr. Katz was short and stocky with grey hair and olive skin befitting his Israeli heritage. He had a large nose and curly hair. Many friends commented that he was a Henry Kissinger look alike. Nurses and doctors rushed back and forth ministering what aid and comfort they could, while the cries and coughs of patients added to the cacophony of ambulance sirens bringing in new patients and doctors shouting instructions to harried nurses.

All of the medical staff was wearing surgical gloves and masks to avoid exposure to an unknown but extremely contagious virus. Thomas maneuvered his way through the crowded hallway and reached his office, but before he could escape a nurse caught his arm. Ruth Nixon stopped the Doctor and with her clear blue eyes filled with tears earnestly turned him to face her. "Doctor, we've lost another one. First Alice Ryvers, and now Jim Shellenger has succumbed. This is happening too fast, we've got to help these people! What can we do?" Nurse Nixon cried.

"First of all, relax, and take a breath Ruth. You need to calm down and rely on your training. Yes, this is an unusually prolific virus, but it doesn't help to overreact! I need your help to set an example for the other nurses, and for the patients. They need to see your professional demeanor or they will panic as well. Can I rely on you, Ruth?" Thomas said softly, trying to sooth her with his voice and demeanor.

Somewhat calmer Ruth went on, "Yes, Doctor. I'm so sorry. It's just I've never seen anything like this before. All my training and experience didn't prepare me for anything of this scale. There must be forty patients, all showing the same symptoms. What should I do?"

"Comfort and contain, Nurse Nixon. That's all we can do until we know what we're dealing with. The Metropolitan Medical Strike Team has been activated. The hospital has been quarantined and we have to maintain biohazard procedures until further notice. Only those patients with the symptoms of this new virus will be admitted and clinics will have to handle emergency patients with other injuries. I need to contact the National Center for Infectious Disease and ask for their help. Please, do the best you can and spread the word. We're in this for the long haul Ruth. Can I depend on you?" Thomas concluded and squeezed her arm.

Nurse Nixon nodded softly, took a deep breath, and squared her shoulders. She was thankful for the assurance and for the comfort his touch gave her. She turned and walked quickly back into the fray.

Thomas entered his office just as his phone rang. "What now!" he said annoyed and picked up the phone. "Thomas Katz." He said brusquely whipping off his surgical mask.

"Dr. Katz, this is Melinda Chase from CDC. We've been alerted to an incident in Seattle and wondered if you could give us any more details?"

"Really? I was just going to call you. We need some help here. We are getting more patients every hour showing the same symptoms. Our hospitals are becoming overcrowded and MMST has been activated. We are treating this as a WMD incident until we find out the cause of the contagion." Thomas declared referring to the Weapons of Mass Destruction scenario they all trained for since 9/11.

"Have you had any casualties?" Melinda asked.

"Unfortunately, yes. Alice Ryvers. A pretty 9 year old girl succumbed to the disease this morning. Another man in his sixties, Jim Shellenger, just died a few minutes ago."

"How are you coping Thomas? Can you arrange an autopsy? We need a blood and tissue sample to help identify the active agent." Melinda asked.

"Yes, of course our medical examiner will be able to get on it right away. We have initiated biohazard procedures and quarantine is in effect. The police have closed off the block around the hospital and no one is getting in unless they are first screened by Emergency Medical staffs that have set up triage outside. However, we are getting new patients every hour and the halls are full. We are evacuating the second floor ICU patients to higher floors to make room, but we'll soon be overrun. I haven't seen anything of this scale since my time in Vietnam." Thomas said exasperated.

"Hang in there Thomas. We'll get some answers for you as soon as we can analyze the samples you send us. If you could expedite the package it would help immensely." Melinda said.

"No problem Melinda. We appreciate the help. I'll send it out by helicopter to Sea-Tac and charter a medical jet to fly it out to you within the hour. You should get it in about ten hours. Thanks again, goodbye"

"Good luck Dr. Katz. Let us know if there is anything else we can do."

"Pray" Thomas said and hung up.

Chapter 14

Matthew Parker drove along the coast of California in his Crossfire. The wind blew through his hair as he weaved in and out of traffic. He wasn't thinking about how nice the car handled, or how beautiful the view. His mind was on the death of Rebecca Forster, and the man responsible. Matt found it hard to believe that Doctor Magee would jeopardize his own career for the sake of avarice, not to mention the significant benefits to mankind that his nanobots could achieve. What kind of a man, a doctor yet, would do this? Matt thought to himself. All the hard work, the late nights and the effort to get FDA approval to conduct human testing was for nothing. With the death of Rebecca Forster, Matt would lose any credibility in the Medical Community. Instead of being a hero, he would be known as a villain, even a murderer.

Matt continued along the Cabrillo Highway until he reached the exit to Tunitas Creek Road. The Doctor lived on a private road off Tunitas Creek road, in a nice house appropriate for a man of his status in the community and with his position at the University.

Matt pulled up to the security gate and buzzed the intercom. "Yes?" a woman's voice answered with a slightly Spanish accent. "Hi Monique, it's Matt Parker." Matt said.

"Oh, Matthew, please come in!" Doctor Magee's wife exclaimed and released the gate from a button inside the house.

The gate swung open and Matt drove up the tree lined drive, around a circular green and pulled up to the house. He jumped out of the car and walked toward the house. The Magee house was a California special. It had only one story and sprawled over 16000 square feet with a central courtyard. Thick stucco walls decorated with plants of every kind were visible from the front and colonnades held up a clay tile roof on both sides of the entry way. There was a gated entrance to the house with carved mahogany double doors inside. Light sprayed from the open door as Monique walked out to open the wrought iron gate. She was dressed in a flowing satin skirt and a silk blouse and it was obvious that she took care of herself. She was wearing a lot of gold as usual. Hoop earrings, a gold necklace and diamonds graced her wrists and fingers. Her long dark hair was tied back in a matching scarf and a smile lit up her face as she welcomed Matthew to her home.

"Matthew, it's so good to see you. It's been too long!" she said as she took his arm in hers and steered him inside.

"Thank you Monique. It's good to see you again too. You are looking as beautiful as ever." Matt said honestly. It was difficult to resist her smile and her natural charm. Matt liked her immensely. She was always a gracious hostess and had a ready smile and reminded him of his own mother.

"We weren't expecting you. Will you stay for dinner? I can set an extra plate!" Monique asked sincerely.

"No thank you Monique, I won't be staying very long. I just came to see Francis for a few minutes." Matt answered quickly.

"Are you sure? I know you like my paella." Monique tried again.

"You know if I could I would, but I can't stay tonight. How about a rain check?"

"Of course. Are you OK Matthew? You don't seem like yourself."

"I'm fine Monique, just something on my mind that I need to discuss with Francis. You understand I hope."

"Yes, yes. I know, your upset about the tragic death this morning, Francis told me. I am so sorry Matt, I wasn't thinking."

"It's OK Monique, ningún problema" No problem said Matt.

They walked arm in arm down the hall to the study where Monique knocked quietly, then opened the door. "Francis, Matthew dropped in to see you."

As the door opened Doctor Magee had his back to the door and he was on the phone. Surprised, turned his head towards them, then back again as he said into the phone "I'll call you later." and hung up. He looked annoyed, but then his countenance changed magically as he smiled and walked to greet them.

"Matthew, what a surprise! Come, sit down. Some coffee perhaps?"

"Yes, that would be nice." Matt said thinking that it would be a good distraction for Monique and would give them some privacy. Matt wasn't looking forward to this confrontation, but knew he couldn't let the doctor get away with murder. He shook the Doctor's hand coolly, and sat down opposite his desk in a leather chair. Francis sat down at his desk and leaned back. Monique left the room quietly and closed the door.

"What's on your mind Matt? It's not like you to drive out this way for nothing and you look terrible. It's Rebecca isn't it? It's not your fault, you know. Poor Rebecca. I did everything I could, but to no avail I'm afraid. I feel just awful. Do you have any idea what happened?" Francis asked. He was a good actor, he even sounds sincere, Matt thought to himself.

"Yes, I think I do. Although, I think you know *exactly* what happened, don't you Doctor?" Matt said with acid in his voice.

"What? What are you talking about?" Francis asked as the color faded from his face, knowing exactly what Matt was saying but unsure *how* he could know.

"I had Rebecca's blood analyzed." Matt said.

"Of course you did. That's normal when a patient dies. I am sure you found nothing unusual. The nanobots wouldn't leave any trace of the damage they caused. I suspect it was a spinal injury causing heart paralysis as a result of your nanobots being over aggressive in that area." The Doctor shook his head sadly. His color returning as he regained his composure.

"Her blood contained an unusual substance. It took some doing but the folks at Berkley Medicine have an excellent lab. They found traces of venom from the Chironex Fleckeri, commonly known as the Sea Wasp. It caused a shutdown of her vital organs and stopped her heart." Matt said

"Ridiculous!" said the Doctor.

"I don't suppose you know how that might have entered her system, Doctor?" Matt asked with a cynical tone.

"What are you suggesting Matthew?" the Doctor said his voice raising in undisguised offence.

"I am not suggesting anything. I know what you did and I am not going to let you get away with it Francis. I am going to the authorities as soon as I leave here to report what I know. I am not going to let you ruin years of work for the sake of greed." Matt said angrily.

"You cannot prove anything. That venom could have been administered by Nurse Fuentes or the equipment could have been tampered with. There are any number of explanations and suspects, including you Matthew. Going to the authorities will not help poor Rebecca." The doctor insisted.

"Her murderer will be brought to justice. I guarantee you that!" Matt said and stood to leave.

"Matthew, Matthew, you always do overreact! Sit down, let's talk about this. I'm sure we can work out an amicable arrangement." The doctor said condescendingly not realizing that by doing so he was admitting his guilt.

"Don't think you can talk me out of this Francis. I'm not interested in your blood money! I'll see that you pay for the murder of Rebecca Forster." Matt said as he turned and headed for the door.

"Matthew, I hope you realize the danger you are putting yourself in. These people do not fool around. Please, reconsider." the doctor pleaded as he walked out from behind his desk, more worried about himself than Matt. If word got out that Gerald Pharmaceuticals had paid him off, his life would be worthless.

"Are you threatening me?" Matt said

"No, dear boy, I'm just advising caution." The doctor said with a smile and clutched Matt's arm.

"Don't waste my time." Matt said, shrugging easily out of the doctor's grip and opened the study door.

Monique was walking towards the study with a tray in her hand. "Matthew, leaving so soon?"

"Yes Monique, I'm so sorry. Thanks for your hospitality." Matt walked by her and left by the front door. He was in his car and speeding out of the driveway when Francis and Monique came to the door and watched him leave.

"He seemed quite upset darling." Monique observed.

"Nothing to worry about Amor." Francis said and squeezed her shoulder. "He will be fine. He's just terribly upset about poor Rebecca's death. He'll get over it."

The doctor returned to his study and picked up the phone. He dialed a familiar number and a man's voice answered. "Yes?"

"We have a problem." The doctor said.

Chapter 15

The rain had been falling for hours now. The South American storm front had blown in from the Pacific earlier that day and was showing no signs of weakening. The ESO Observatory was atop Cerro Paranal, a 2,635-m high mountain, about 120 km south of the town of Antofagasta and 12 km inland from the Pacific Coast. With no source of water other than the rainfall, the observatory held a reservoir of rain water and a treatment facility to purify the liquid.

Derek Manheim had just finished with a class on operating the VLTI telescope with his student researchers. Seven men and four women were working through their undergraduate studies in Astronomy from the Universidad Catolica del Norte in Antofagasta, and from the Ohio State University of Astronomy in Columbus. Derek noticed several of the students had come down with a flu bug and were coughing throughout the demonstration. It was somewhat distracting during the class and Derek wondered what kind of flu bug it was. He wasn't too worried about it though, because his constitution was such that he often avoided the bugs that went around the observatory. Often times he would be the only one not sick when the close quarters of the facility acted like a crucible of infection.

Derek finished up a conversation with one student, Emily Anderson, who didn't look good at all.

"Thanks for the excellent demo Derek, I learned a lot. When do we get hands on?" Emily asked.

"In a couple of days I will start one-on-one training." Derek answered.

"I…" Emily coughed, and then sneezed,"…am looking forward to one-on-one with you Derek" she said trying to be seductive, but not succeeding with her red eyes and ragged cough.

"Yes, me too Emily. I'll see you later." said Derek stepping back to avoid the spray. Emily smiled, moved a stray hair from her face and headed for the door. Before she reached the door, however, she doubled over in a deep coughing spell, straightened and left.

"Maybe when you're better sweetheart." Derek said sardonically.

Derek walked across the compound under the covered walkway to the VLTI control room where his desk was located. He rolled up his collar against wind and rain as he walked and he observed several workers heading to the infirmary. They were in groups of two or three, helping each other along. They didn't seem to notice that they were getting soaked. "What is going on?" he thought to himself. "This is serious!" Derek picked up his pace a bit. When he arrived at his desk he picked up his wireless phone and said into the mouthpiece "Frederick Schoefield." After a short pause Frederick answered. "Schoefield."

"Fred, have you noticed the flu bug going around?" Derek asked concerned.

"How did you know? I don't feel so well myself."

"Are you sick as well?"

"Yes Derek, I am. I've been feeling a little under the weather since breakfast. I thought it was something I ate. I still haven't got used to the local diet. You'd think I would after all this time."

"I don't think it's the food Fred. I noticed that several of my student researchers were coughing this morning during the training session, and there were several workers heading to the infirmary. I think we might have an flu bug on our hands."

"Hmm, I'll look into it. I'll call the Doctor and see what's going on."

"OK. Let me know if I can help."

"Absolutely, out." said Frederick and hung up.

Derek sat down at his desk and looked over the logs for the day. Nothing much new and exciting was happening. After the Manheim Meteor, named after him, things were going to be anti-climactic. Derek got up and walked to the window. The rain was beating against the window and rivulets of water were forming on the ground. He could see more people heading to the infirmary. The Doctor must be overwhelmed he thought to himself.

The infirmary was indeed getting full. Doctor Angela Zamora was becoming anxious. Several patients were already in the few dozen beds they had and more were coming in every minute. All were showing the same symptoms; shortness of breath, ragged cough, weakness, sinus congestion and redness in the eyes. A couple of the worst ones were coughing up blood. She was doing what she could for them but they were not showing any response to antibiotics. All she could do was make them comfortable for now. There were only seventy five at the facility and twenty two were in the infirmary at last count.

The first patient in was a student named Thomas from the University in Antofagasta. He started coughing again and couldn't stop. Angela rushed to his bedside and donned a mask and gloves. She pulled a curtain around the bed to reduce the tension in the open ward and she tried to calm him down but to no avail. She administered a sedative through the I.V. line but instead of relaxing him, he coughed even more and stopped breathing. Soon after, his heart stopped. Angela tried to resuscitate him but he died with a grotesque look on his face. His tongue was distended and his eyes swollen. Angela cried out in frustration "What is going on!" She covered his body with a sheet, sat on the end of his bed and removed her gloves and mask. Feeling helpless and moved to tears she sobbed quietly in the privacy of the makeshift room.

A nurse with Flora on her name tag rushed to her and opened the curtain, "Doctor, another patient is in trouble, come quickly!"

Doctor Zamora gathered her composure quickly, wiped away the tears and followed the nurse to a bed across the room. A young woman was bleeding from the nose and coughing profusely. She was panicking as her breathing was difficult and she couldn't stop coughing. Her wide eyes showed her fear as the Doctor methodically checked her over while trying to ease her panic. In her haste Doctor Zamora neglected to put on her mask and gloves. As the Doctor was looking in the patients eyes with a scope, the patient coughed raggedly and blood tainted saliva sprayed on the Doctors face, entering her eyes and mouth. The Doctor cursed and quickly wiped her face with her uncovered hands. Realizing her exposure the Doctor rushed to a sink and washed herself with disinfectant soap, hoping she had acted in time.

The patient stopped coughing and Doctor Zamora turned to see another face from a nightmare. The patient had expired with the same look of terror and grotesque tongue protruding from her mouth. "This is insane!" She thought to herself. I need to get help. "Cover her up please." She instructed the nurse, then she walked down the hall to her office and over to her desk. She opened her address book and found the number for the Minister of Health for the Segunda Region, Enriquez Novoas. She placed the call.

"May I speak with the Director please, this is Doctor Angela Zamora from the Paranal Observatory. Yes this is an emergency!" the Doctor said urgently.

"Hola?" answered Doctor Novoas.

"Doctor Novoas, this is Angela Zamora from the ESO observatory. I have need of immediate assistance. I have several cases of an unknown virus infecting half of the staff here. I have had two fatalities already and nothing I do seems to have any effect. Can you send help?" Angela asked intensely.

"Please, please, Doctor, I understand your predicament. I am afraid you are not alone, however. I have had reports from all over the region of a similar virus at work. I am working with our Emergency Response Division to organize quarantine and medical help to everyone possible. It is impossible to say at this time when we can assist you. Hospitals in Antogafasta are inundated with victims of this strange new virus and I am sorry to say that we have had no better success than you. Our best minds are examining this virus, but it is unlike anything we have seen before. It does not respond to traditional or radical antibiotics or antiviral medication."

"But Doctor Novoas, my patients are dying! Surely there is something you can do."

"I am so sorry Doctor Zamora. Please be careful. We do not yet know how this is transmitted. You must make sure that biohazard procedures are followed to the letter. In particular, you must make sure that the bodies are isolated and enclosed in secure polypropylene bags. Until we know how the virus is transmitted, we cannot let the bodies be exposed to the air."

Angela touched her face carefully and wiped her lips as she thought about her exposure to the last victim. "Of course Doctor, I, I understand" she said hesitantly. "Thank you. Please send help as soon as you can."

"Yes, of course Angela. God be with you." said Doctor Novoas and hung up. Before she could turn around to leave the phone rang. "Zamora." She answered.

"Doctor, this is Frederick Schoefield. I am not feeling very well, I was wondering if I could come down to the infirmary to see you if you have the time?" Fred asked.

"Frederick, I am overwhelmed with patients right now. There seems to be some kind of virus at work and I have every bed full. I think we have an epidemic on our hands. Unless you get any worse I wouldn't recommend you come down here. I want to contain the spread if I can."

"Oh, I see. It's that serious?"

"I am afraid so, Frederick. I have spoken to the Ministry of Health and it's not just us. The hospitals are inundated with patients showing the same symptoms. I asked for help, but they don't know when they can get to us. I recommend that you make an announcement to warn the rest of the staff to avoid contact with those infected and to stay in their rooms until further notice."

"You are recommending that I quarantine the facility?"

"Yes, Frederick. I am."

"Very well. I'll make the announcement right away. Thank you Doctor. Are you alright?"

"I am doing the best I can under the circumstances. We'll cope until help arrives"

"Very good Doctor. Schoefield out!"

Doctor Zamora hung up the phone and returned to the ward. Patients were in every bed and several others were demanding attention. Doctor Zamora took a deep steadying breath and went to work.

"Attention! Attention! This is Frederick Schoefield. We have an emergency situation. There appears to be a virus at work in our facility. Please remain in your rooms until further notice. We are invoking a quarantine of all

personnel. Please avoid contact with others and please do not leave the facility. Doctor Zamora is treating only those patients with symptoms. Please do not go to the infirmary unless symptoms occur. Help has been requested from the Ministry of Health and we expect their arrival at any time. I appreciate your cooperation. Schoefield out!"

Frederick replaced the microphone to the PA system and sat heavily in the closest chair. He removed his glasses with his left hand and pinched the bridge of his nose with the thumb and forefinger of his right hand. He really wasn't feeling very well at all. His cough had been getting progressively worse as the day went on and he was very tired. His breathing was rough and he tried to catch his breath and relax. Out of his pocket he pulled a cough drop from a pack he had purchased earlier that day with the intent of relieving his sore throat and annoying cough but before he could get it into his mouth he started on another coughing spell.

He stood anxiously and doubled over with the effort of coughing and couldn't quite get his breath. Tumbling to the floor he crawled towards his desk hoping to call for help. His nose started bleeding and pooled on the floor below him. He crawled through it in a determined effort, but he was soon overcome by the lack of oxygen as his lungs lost their ability to take air. He reached his desk and stretched out his hand desperately for the phone to call for help. Unfortunately for Frederick he collapsed before he could reach it. Lying in a pool of his own blood, he thought of his dear departed wife and could see her spreading her arms in welcome, smiling at him, waiting, and then Frederick Schoefield breathed his last breath.

Chapter 16

The Beechcraft King Air 350 received it's clearance to land at Atlanta Hartsfield International Airport. The pilot turned on the landing lights, reduced speed, lowered flaps and gear, and then lined up the approach. With a top speed of 240 knots the ten hour flight went without a hitch missing weather systems and refueling in Chicago to make the trip. The pilot touched down on the numbers and taxied off the runway. Switching to ground clearance and delivery he requested taxi instructions. The ground traffic controller gave directions to the South terminal, and he was told that an ambulance was waiting for his cargo there. After arriving at the South terminal the pilot powered down his engines and opened the main exit door. An ambulance screeched to a stop a few feet away and two burly paramedics approached the airplane. The pilot carefully carried the small cooler with biohazard symbols an all sides down the exit stairs and passed it off to the paramedics. With a quick salute and a thank you the men entered their vehicle and rushed off into the distance, sirens blaring as they went. The pilot headed for the nearest lounge.

The ambulance took off out of the Airport exit onto South Terminal Parkway then onto Airport Boulevard. Exiting onto North Terminal Parkway the ambulance then took the ramp to I-85 North to Atlanta. Cars pulled off to the right to let the Emergency Vehicle pass and the ambulance was soon at exit 248C to Carter Center. A couple of turns later and it pulled up to CDC headquarters on Clifton Road North East. A security guard greeted them and the package was delivered to the front entrance. Noah

Drew was there to sign for the package which he took immediately up to the lab.

Noah entered the lab and placed the sample case down. Donning biohazard garb, complete with oxygen tank, Noah picked up the case and headed into the clean room. Two double doors opened automatically and let him into a closed room with another set of double doors in the rear. Once the first set of doors closed, there was a hiss of air being exchanged as the rooms environment adjusted to that of the clean room and then the rear doors opened allowing Noah to enter the lab.

Once inside Noah went to a desk in the center of the room. After placing the case on the desk he broke the biohazard seal and opened it. Inside was a sealed metal box. Noah took the box and placed it inside a Plexiglas containment tank that looked like a fish tank, but with gloved openings in the side. Also inside were a variety of tools used to examine toxic substances. Closing the top of the tank Noah placed his hands inside the gloved openings and began his work.

Cautiously opening the metal box Noah saw inside several samples of organ tissue removed from the body of the elderly man, and a vial of blood. He first took the vial opened it. Then with a dropper removed a little blood and placed it on a glass slide. After closing the vial, Noah placed the glass slide into a device that looked much like a microscope, but without an eye-piece.

After removing himself from the containment tank gloves, Noah walked over to a computer console and began typing on the keyboard. On a flat screen monitor he could see the blood sample quite clearly. Using the computer he changed the magnification and he could see individual red and white blood cells along with several other unidentified virus like cells. Changing the magnification again, he focused in on one of the viruses.

The virus was round like many viruses but it had a rainbow of colors covering the surface. Most viruses are colored, some with more than one or even three colors but this one seemed to change color as Noah watched, much like oil on the surface of water. "That's unique." Noah said out loud. The virus had many spiked protrusions on its surface, with little barbs on the end that could attach to tissue much like some seeds attach to the socks   weary hikers.

Noah typed a new command into the computer. Data overlaid the image showing the number of viruses in the sample, the blood count and platelet count. There were plenty of viruses in the sample so he could begin testing antivirus drugs against it. Before he continued, he pressed a button on the speakerphone at the desk and dialed Jacob's local. After a couple of rings Jacob answered. "Jacob, its Noah. I'm in the lab looking at the sample that's just arrived from Seattle. There is a new virus at work here. It is unlike anything I've seen before. Do you want to have a look?" he asked.

"Sure Noah. Can you send over an image?" Jacob asked in reply.

"OK. I'll also run it against our CDC database and see if the computer can find a match. Do you think we should begin testing on live hosts to see the results of exposure for ourselves?"

"Not yet, let's run it by Melinda and wait for the computer analysis first."

"OK, no problem. I'll have a look at the tissue samples next."

"Sounds good, I'd like to hear what you find."

"Absolutely, bye."

"Bye"

Noah focused his attention on the computer screen. Typing commands on the keyboard he changed the filters used on the sample. As he moved through the spectrum he snapped photographs that were automatically saved with a new catalog and series number. Next he walked back to the containment tank and placed his hands in the tank gloves. He then picked up a syringe of dye and added it to the sample on the microscope glass.

Going back to the computer he saw that the dye had an immediate effect on the sample, cell walls became better defined, and the contrasts of the entire image improved, and when Noah changed from a color to monochrome lens the image became incredibly clear.

Noah started on another slew of photographs adding to the catalog. When he was done there were over one hundred new photos of the virus and it's effect on the cells around it. One advantage of taking so many photos was that when they were reviewed one after the other it was like watching a time-lapse movie. He could see with microscopic detail a virus attacking, penetrating and occupying a healthy cell. He could watch as the virus fed off the cytoplasm and attacked the nucleus and finally altered the cell's DNA so that it produced more viruses. When the cell could no longer contain the new corrupted cells, it ruptured and the process began again.

Noah saved all the images and went back to the containment tank and opened a tissue sample. Using surgical instruments already inside the tank he precisely sliced off a small piece of liver tissue and placed it on a slide and put it under the microscope.

Looking again at the monitor he could see the sample at great magnification but it needed to be brighter, so he increased the illumination. Snapping photographs as he went he manipulated the sample with a variety of sharp tools so that he could get the best pictures possible. When he was done, he walked over to the computer and initiated a database search against each picture.

The search was the work of Sam who created it to work much like a fingerprint match program, but it used the virus profile as the search criteria, along with the images of the virus. Noah entered everything he had discovered about the virus so far, and submitted the query. The computer screen started matching virus photos against photos in the database at lightning speed. If a match was found the results would be sent, at Noah's request, to each member of the team.

While that was running, Noah went back to the containment tank and began testing of the virus against the standard stream of anti-virals. It would be a long evening.

Chapter 17

Lieutenant Colonel John Reed was driving his customized 1976 Jeep Wagoneer East on I-90 across the E. Channel Bridge on his way to his home near Issaquah, Washington. He liked things made in the USA and especially classic automobiles. His Jeep had a modified AMC V8 engine with 510hp and could be considered a sleeper by those who like fast cars. It looked old and tired but it could outperform many cars in power on and off road.

John was listening to the oldies station on the radio. He loved the music but it irritated him that sixties and seventies, even eighties music was considered oldies. At 54 he wasn't old. At least he didn't feel old.

Col. Reed was a retired Marine, 'Semper Fi' being their motto for life, meaning 'always faithful'. Once a Marine always a Marine was also a common saying and Marines live by a code of excellence, and loyalty to one another and to the country that permeates every area of their life.

He still had the same physique that he had when he joined the marines at 18, although he was probably even stronger and leaner than he was then after 25 years of service to his country.

John stayed in shape with a daily routine that started at 04:30 am every morning. By the time most people were getting out of bed to get ready for work he had already run ten miles, completed a regime of calisthenics, finished his breakfast, showered and dressed.

As he drove through the heavy rain along the highway he could barely see Lake Sammamish on his left and Cougar Mountain beginning to rise on his right. Rain was nothing uncommon to residents of the Pacific Northwest and John was prepared. He was was wearing a rain poncho and a jungle boonie hat in green camouflage.

His house backed Cougar Mountain on the south side and the State park of the same name provided miles of trails and forest to hike in whenever he was in the mood.

After the Marine Corps, John worked as a strategic consultant to the Moderation Services Corporation or MSC. MSC was an organization that supplied special services to the Military, to the CIA, to the FBI or to Homeland Security. These special services included security, skills training, military operations and strategy, and special operations. Spec. Ops. As they were commonly known among those involved, were usually 'top secret' missions and anyone outside the hiring organization and MSC were not privy to the details of those missions. The House Oversight Committee investigated MSC involvement in the Iraq War but there was no evidence of wrong doing. Operations for the CIA and Homeland security were more secretive and unknown to the media, or the public, which was probably a good thing.

John was a sought out resource to MSC clients. Although he was a professional soldier and could hold his own in combat situations, his forte was military strategy and planning. He thought on his feet and could picture in his mind the entire campaign as it happened, and make necessary adjustments that worked. He could plan multiple scenarios for an operation and limit casualties to both sides to accomplish the objective.

John was an avid reader of military history. His extensive library contained some good books like 'The American Soldier' by General Tommy Franks, 'The Army of the Future' by General Charles De Gaulle, 'The Art of War' by Sung Shi and even the Bible.

John turned onto the Renton-Issaquah highway and then onto 158th Avenue SE and finally onto his road, SE 102nd Street. The forest lined road formed a canopy overhead and blocked out the sun at the best of times, but today it was dark and foreboding. The paved road gave way to gravel about half way up the steep grade to his house, where it continued until a final curve in the road when the trees parted to reveal his rustic estate.

Once through the reinforced steel gate that was already open, John pulled around to the backside of his four car garage. The doors were in back because John preferred to keep the vehicles he owned hidden from public view when the doors were opened.

He parked his Jeep in the first door and got out. A quick and habitual check of his other vehicles revealed no tampering that he could see. His military Humvee still painted in desert tan, his Ford F350 4x4 Diesel, and his Harley Davidson Fat Boy all shared the space with his Jeep Wagoneer.

He had two Honda four wheel ATV's in the barn that was full of camping gear, rock climbing gear, and an underground weapons and food cache that he told very few people about.

Twirling his keys in his hand he walked towards his back door and pivoted his head back and forth as he went. John didn't even realize he was doing it. His training had become such a part of his life that even if he wanted to he couldn't ignore his surroundings. Instantly his senses were engaged as he noticed motion in the trees to his right. He began to whistle as he continued to walk towards his house he casually reached inconspicuously for his concealed Browning 1911.

John heard a crunch of gravel behind him through the noise of the rain falling in the trees. Dropping his keys, he pivoted on his heel, drew his handgun from under his rain poncho and had the intruder in his sights from a crouched position in less time than it took for his keys to hit the ground.

John relaxed and stood up as he recognized Sergeant Cornelius Quinn. "Connie" he said lowering his weapon and holstering it under his poncho.

"Colonel, I had you this time, Boyo!" Connie said with a grin, lowering his own weapon, a H&K MP5.

"Maybe you did Connie, maybe you did." John said with a smile, turning towards the house. Connie followed behind him.

They entered his home through the back door which brought them into John's kitchen. The simple home fit John perfectly and its decor reflected his personality now. Since his wife died eight years ago in a car accident, John did little entertaining. His son John and his daughter Alyssa were both married and grown, living their own lives now with little time for Dad.

John understood how they felt because he blamed himself for his wife's death. She went out in their own Chevy Malibu to get some groceries. John hadn't checked the vehicle that night when he came home and someone had tampered with the brakes to get back at John. His wife Lori had paid the price.

Throwing his keys on the table he reached the security system and turned off the house alarm. Connie took of his boonie and poncho and hung them on the wall by the back door. John hung his in the laundry room and returned with two beers from the extra fridge where he kept his supply. "Here you go Connie" John said as he handed one to his friend he'd met at MSC.

Sergeant Cornelius "Connie" Patrick Quinn (retired) hailed from his native Ireland and retired from the Irish Army.

This little known force began during the Irish Civil war in the 1920's. During the Second World War Ireland remained mostly neutral, although it had some role in the capturing of the German spy Hermman Gortz, and securing German prisoners in a camp at Curragh in County Kildare, Ireland.

Ireland joined the UN in 1955 and since then the Irish Army has been involved in 'peacekeeping' missions around the world.

John and Connie met in Iraq where 171 of his countrymen were deployed to supervise the withdrawal of Iranian and Iraqi troops.

Few people knew, however, of the 6 elite Irish Army soldiers and 6 US Navy SEALS who as a team successfully stopped the Iraqi missile attacks on 'reflagged' US tankers, and who blew up several Iraqi owned oil rigs in the Strait of Hormuz in 1987. The UN sanctioned mission was planned and executed by one young Lieutenant John Reed.

"Thanks Boyo." Connie said.

"So," John began, "What are you doing here Connie. I thought you were on vacation in Hawaii?"

"The weather there was worse than here! Look at that mess!" Connie said gesturing out the window. "I went for some R&R and some beach time and got rusty instead. I booked a flight home and here I am. I figured you could use some company to shake up this old house."

"What do you mean?" asked John, suspiciously.

"The boys are coming over. I figured we'd play some paintball in the back forty if the rain clears up. Hone our skills as it were." Connie laughed. "If not, we'll just grill some steaks and drink your beer!"

"Have you forgotten that this is my house you Irish drunkard! It doesn't need shaking up." John said only half tongue in cheek.

"Now, John, don't be takin' that tone wi'me! After the meteor didn't end the world we could all use a little celebration. It'll be fun! Besides, you've been moping around this house far too long. She's been gone eight years, now son."

"I know how long she's been dead Cornelius. You don't have to tell me."

"Well, then, let's have some fun! The boys'll be here any minute."

"Fine. I suppose you are right Connie. It could have all ended yesterday huh?" John said.

"That's the Spirit!" Connie said as he reached into his pocket and pressed the button on the side of his cell phone and said, "All clear!"

From the trees came apparitions in camouflaged outfits. They appeared out of nowhere, and the untrained eye would never have seen them. Vehicles pulled out of the bushes and rolled to a stop in the back driveway.

Connie's boys were eleven elite soldiers, the same ones who had been deployed in the Gulf War. Some were still in the service, others had retired as well, many worked for MSC on occasion, and all were friends for life; Brothers in arms.

Weapons were secured, hats and coats hung up, coolers carried, and bags set down in John's kitchen. It was time to celebrate again. Not that the men needed an excuse. Each one saluted, then greeted John, shook his hand and was given hug, a beer and a smile in return.

It was early afternoon and soon steaks were sizzling and laughter was heard to echo in the halls of the house where laughter hadn't been heard for some time.

Chapter 18

Matthew Parker was heading for the Oakland Police Department and was negotiating the curves of the scenic tree-lined Skyline Boulevard when a black Cadillac Escalade kept riding his tail, flashing its high beams and seemed to want to pass. Matt had put up his convertible top at the Magees when it looked like rain and didn't notice the SUV at first and the Crossfire's rear view wasn't the greatest with the top up. As the sun was setting Matt turned on his lights and stepped on the gas. The Crossfire leaped forward in response to the engine's throaty roar and the headlights of the Escalade were left far behind.

After three curves the road straightened out for a mile or so giving the Escalade a chance to catch up to the Crossfire. This time the Escalade driver made his intentions clear. As the SUV got close to the Crossfire, the driver gunned the engine and rammed the Crossfire from behind sending the car into a fish-tail.

Matt was surprised by the aggressive move but was quickly able to regain control of the smaller sports car, using the skills he had learned pushing the limits of the Crossfire on winding roads just like this one. "What are you doing?" Matt yelled to his rear view mirror. "Are you crazy?!"

Shifting down and accelerating again, Matt put some distance between him and the SUV. The 400hp v8 engine of the Cadillac Escalade easily out powered the Chrysler Crossfires 300hp v6, but if Matt could make it to the curves he could out maneuver the SUV because of the lower profile and nimble handling of the Crossfire.

The SUV gunned his engine and hit the sports car again from behind. Matt was ready this time and hit the gas as the SUV crashed into him, minimizing the impact and keeping control of the car.

Matt saw flashes behind him and when his tiny rear window blew out, he realized that someone was leaning out of the passenger window of the SUV and firing at him with a fully automatic machine pistol. Bullets stitched a path across the convertible top but miraculously missed Matt's head by inches. "Enough of this!" Matt said out loud. Matt slowed the Crossfire and eased the car onto the shoulder of the road coming to a stop. The SUV followed suit.

Taking a chance that the men in the car would not open fire as soon as he stood up, Matt exited the vehicle, hands in the air, and faced his pursuers.

Two men came out of the Escalade carrying Heckler and Koch MP5's wearing black suits and ties. They looked like twins, both had a military bearing and brush cuts, and sun glasses. Except for their height, they were cut from the same mold.

Matt asked "What do you want?"

Neither spoke as they approached Matt, guns pointed at his stomach.

"Seriously, if you guys wanted to pass me there was ample opportunity a mile back" Matt said tongue in cheek.

"Shut up!" said the shorter of the two, obviously the leader.

"OK, OK, but what is the problem?" Matt asked as he started to walk slowly towards them.

"Don't move and Shut up!" the leader commanded, louder this time.

Matt stopped walking, smiling and lower his hands at the same time. The men were now within a few feet of Matt. He examined them closer. Definitely military trained, he thought, maybe mercenaries now, paid by Gerald Pharmaceuticals? "How good were they?" He thought. "Did they really want to kill him, or just scare him?" He'd find out soon enough.

The leader looked back to the SUV and nodded his head. The rear door opened and a man stepped out.

He was wearing a trench coat and a panama hat. A cigar was in his mouth, it had been used but was now unlit. He had a powerful build and walked confidently forward until he was between his men, but behind them.

"Mr. Parker! It's such a pleasant evening for a drive. I'm so sorry you had car trouble." Jennings said sarcastically.

"Who are you?" Matt asked.

"That's not important, Mr. Parker. What's important is that you understand what I have to say."

"And what's that?"

"Poor Rebecca died for a good cause. Because of her death, people will continue to donate to Cancer research. Federal Grants will still be issued to dedicated research foundations and universities, and many, many drugs will be sold benefiting thousands of cancer patients every year, giving them hope!"

"That's crap and you know it. Rebecca died because Dr. Magee killed her! You obviously work for Gerald Pharmaceuticals." Matt said.

A look of surprise was quickly hidden from Jennings face as he said "Who I work for is unimportant. What is important is that you stop travelling this dangerous road that you are on." A smile touched his face as he realized the unintentional pun. He continued.

"Please, for your safety, do not speak to the police about Rebecca's sudden, but expected death. I would also suggest you stay away from Dr. Magee. I'd hate to see something happen to him, or his lovely wife." Jennings sucked in a breath. "Oh yes, she is lovely, mmm, mmm, mmm."

"You leave her out of this! She is innocent!" Matt exclaimed.

"Of course, of course, Mr. Parker, but that is up to you, no?"

"If I agree, how do I know you'll leave me and the Magees alone?" Matt asked.

"The alternative is not so pleasant." Jennings nodded once.

Without warning, the taller of the two body guards slammed Matt in the gut with the butt of his machine pistol. Matt doubled over, but only for a moment. On his way back up he used his momentum to build power and with his palm struck the taller man in the jaw with all that he had. This was completely unexpected and the blow lifted the man off his feet. He landed on his back, out cold.

The shorter man's training clicked in and he raised his gun to fire.

Matt expected this of the second body guard however and had already begun his offensive move. He pivoted with the follow-through of his palm strike and ducked, throwing out his left leg knocked the man off his feet.

The gun fired where Matt was, making nice holes in the side of his Crossfire, but missing him. As the man hit the ground his gun flew from his hand. Matt was on him in an instant. One strike to the sternum and the leader was struggling for breath. Another to the side of the neck and he joined his twin in slumber.

Matt looked up to see Jennings getting into the SUV's driver seat and closing the door. The vehicles engine roared to life and Jennings tried to run Matt down with the black behemoth. Matt dove to the side and rolled to avoid the speeding car. When he stood up, all he could see were the taillights disappearing around a curve.

Matt took the guns and a few clips from the twins. He checked their pulses for signs of life and dragged them off the road and onto a grassy bank. Both were alive but would be out for a couple of hours.

"Sorry guys, but you started it!" Matt said to the sleeping men.

Matt got into the Crossfire, started it up and continued on his way to the Oakland Police Department. He picked up his phone and auto-dialed Dr. Magee. As the phone dialed Matt turned on his wipers. It was starting to rain.

Chapter 19

Derek had lost track of time. "KAMY, what time is it?" he asked the AI computer.

"In what time zone, Dr. Manheim?" KAMY responded. Could a computer sound sarcastic? Derek thought.

"This one KAMY."

"It is 5:03 pm local time."

"Wow, I guess I should quit for now."

"Is that a request Dr. Manheim?"

"No KAMY. However, you should probably go on standby and run your backups." Derek said.

"Agreed. I am a little tired myself." KAMY said.

"Can computers get tired?" Derek thought. "I really am tired." He said to himself. Then to KAMY. "OK then, shut down verbal controls. Bye KAMY"

"Shutting down verbal controls. Good night sweetheart."

"Now I'm really hearing things" Derek said to himself.

Derek shut down the consoles, the computer terminals and the lights on his way out the door. It was still raining as he walked out into the covered walkway between the lab and his quarters. There was no one in sight, which wasn't unusual for this time in the evening as most would be heading for the cafeteria. Especially with the self-imposed quarantine by Frederick Schoefield in effect.

Reaching the outer door of the resident apartments, he noticed that there were several lumps of clothes in the hallway. Getting closer, he realized that they were not lumps of clothes but bodies lying on the floor. Some were in the hallway; some were halfway into their apartment doorways. None were moving.

"What is going on?" Derek said out loud. "Hello? Is anybody there?" he called.

There was no response. When He got closer to one of the bodies he saw that it was face down. It was a woman based on the clothes and the hair, but he couldn't see her face. He rolled her over.

He was greeted by a scene from a horror movie. Bulging red and bleeding eyes and a grossly swollen tongue made Emily Anderson barely recognizable.

Derek leaped back in horror. With his back to the wall avoiding the other bodies, he gingerly made his way to his apartment. Using his key he opened the door and once inside he locked and bolted his door.

He needed to think clearly. Derek entered his bathroom, went over to the sink and started the water running. Letting the water wash over his hand he waited for the water to get nice and hot. He pooled the water in his hands as steam began to rise and started to lift his water filled hands to his face.

The phone rang loudly making him jump and spill the water from his hands. He quickly dried his hands on a towel he'd picked up hanging on the wall of his bathroom and ran to the phone. Dropping the towel on the floor he picked up the handset.

"Hello?"

"Hello. Oh thank God! Who is this please?" asked a concerned voice.

"This is Dr. Derek Manheim. Who is this?" Derek asked.

"This is Dr. Enrique Novoas, Minister of Health for the Segunda Region. I have been trying for hours to reach Dr. Zamora. I have tried every number sequence I could think of with the prefix of your facility. Yours is the first to answer."

"Dr. Novoas, what is going on? Everyone here is dead! Bodies are everywhere! They are grossly deformed as well. What happened? Is it a biological attack?"

"We honestly don't know. But one thing we do know. Don't drink the water! Everything points to a water born virus. I hope you haven't touched any bodies. It can be transferred by bodily fluids as well, even after death."

"I did touch one body, but I was careful. Wait a minute, what about chlorinated water? Isn't that safe?" Derek asked, thinking of what he almost did.

"No. In fact we have detected the virus in rainwater, so I would avoid that also. Drink bottled water, it should be safe."

"How am I supposed to avoid rainwater? Our water supply here is from rainwater. Have you looked outside? It's pouring rain right now!" Derek exclaimed.

"I know it has been raining here all day. Listen, can you put me through to Dr. Zamora?" asked Dr. Novoas.

Derek sighed. "OK, I'll try, hang on." Derek pressed the call transfer button on his phone, punched in the number for the clinic and waited for the ringing to stop. When it finally did, he pressed the hook switch and initiated a three way call.

"Hello? Hello!" Derek said.

"Help - me!" was the whispered response followed by a deep raspy coughing spell.

"Who is this? Hello!"

"This is Flora, please help me. They are all dead. We tried to help, but we couldn't! We tried everything! Nothing worked. They're all gone…" her voice fading.

"Flora, this is Dr Novoas. Is Angela there, let me speak with her please." Dr. Novoas said urgently.

"They're all gone." Flora said hopelessly, then went into another coughing spell. Derek and Dr. Novoas listened helplessly as Flora finally stopped coughing.

"Flora!" Derek yelled into the receiver. "Answer me!"

With a muffled thud, the phone landed on the floor and they were disconnected. On the other end of the line, Flora slid down the wall she was resting her back against. Her last vision through bloodshot eyes was that of the infirmary strewn with dead bodies, including the body of Dr. Angela Zamora. Her hand was on the head of a dead female student who was curled up on the lounge chair beside her, and whose head was resting on her lap as Angela sat dead on the chair reserved for waiting patients.

"She's gone. There's nothing we can do for her."

"What about us? Can't you send someone to help?" Derek asked.

"I have no one to send Dr. Manheim. The hospital is now a morgue. There is only a few of us left that are not infected. I have sent an email to the CDC in Atlanta letting them know that the virus is water borne."

"The city is in chaos. Looting has begun. Panic has set in and people are running in confusion. Bodies are lying in the streets. I'm afraid that unless we find some way to fight this thing, the whole region will be decimated. I only hope that this is localized. If it is water borne and in the clouds, it could soon become a worldwide epidemic the likes of which we've never seen before. God help us." Dr. Novoas said morosely.

"There must be something we can do!" Derek exclaimed

"If you think of something, let me know. My number is 55 262 571."

"Sure." Derek said. He hung up and let out a sigh of exhaustion.

Derek tried every line in the Facility. He even tried the PA system. No one answered. He was alone.

Chapter 20

The alien particles were picked up by the polar jet stream and blasted around the world at 275 mph. The subtropical jet stream picked up some of the alien dust and moved it into the Hawaiian Islands and onto Washington State all the way to New York and beyond. With the strong dispersal pattern and the help of the jet stream, in a short time there would be no safe haven on planet Earth.

Chapter 21

Frank Chase was ready to pack it in for the day. He looked at the clock above the view screens and saw that at 5:30 pm and the afternoon shift was already late. He picked up the phone and called Joan Nygaard. When she answered he asked her "Hey Joan, have you seen Bill or Terry yet?"

"Nope." she said. "Haven't they come in yet?"

"No. They are usually on time. Huh." He paused in thought. "Maybe I'll give them a call."

"OK. I can stick around until they get here. I have no plans tonight." Joan said.

"Great, thanks Joan. I'll let you know what I find out." Frank said.

Frank hung up and dialed Bill Swanson's phone number. Bill was a long time employee and as reliable as a Swiss watch. After several tries of his home and cell phone, Frank tried Terry Gellman. When he was about to hang up, Terry answered.

"Yes" he said.

"Terry, it's Frank at work."

"So what do you want?" he asked irritably.

Frank laughed, thinking it was a joke. "Come on Terry! Are you OK? You're late for work, is something up?" Frank asked sincerely.

"Is something up? Are you nuts Frank!" Terry asked incredibly.

"Seriously Terry, what's going on?"

"You really do live in a bubble Frank. Haven't you been watching the news?"

"No, Terry, when would I have time to do that?"

"Oh my, you don't know?"

"Know what Terry? About the meteor? Yes, I knew about that, it was a non-event apparently."

"Not the meteor, the plague! It's on the news! Go home to your family and pray it hasn't hit them yet. Go home Frank!"

"Plague? What are you talking about? Terry?"

Frank heard a dial tone. He hung up the phone and switched the view screen to a local news channel where a newswoman was speaking...

"...*Governor Hansen has declared martial law and no-one is to be on the streets after dark.*"

A pretty young broadcaster, Melody Manson, putting on her best serious face spoke into the camera.

"*President George W Bush has declared a nation-wide restriction on travel in an effort to contain the virus. We are still unclear if this was a biological attack by Muslim extremists in response to the nuclear strike on Iraq earlier today, but it is the common conclusion by experts.*"

The camera switched to an old general in a business suit.

"General Norman Schwarzkopf is here to give his opinion on the possible terrorist attack. General could this have been a biological attack from the Iraqi's?"

"While that is certainly a possibility Melody, I think it would be hasty to jump to that conclusion. The scale and magnitude of the epidemic is greater than any known dispersal mechanism I know of. Remember, it wasn't just the US that is affected. Europe, Australia, Mexico, India, Africa were all hit within the last 24 hours. I have to admit, that with the UN's Multilateral Nonproliferation Agreement on Biological and Chemical Weapons signed several years ago, it would be impossible for any one nation, not even the United States, to attack on this magnitude using anything but nuclear weapons."

"Surely you are not saying this is a natural occurrence, General?"

"Of course I am not Melody. But I am unaware of any other explanation."

"Thank you General Norman Swarzkopf (retired) for your opinions."

"My pleasure Melody!"

"Now to the State Capital, Hartford Connecticut where Governor Hansen is about to speak."

Governor Sam Hansen walked up to the podium inside the State Capital. He was dressed immaculately as usual in a blue business suit and a red power tie. His greying hair was combed to the side and the make-up artist had prepared him for the cameras. Cameras flashed and microphones squealed as all eyes were now on him.

"Thank you all for coming this evening. As you are aware, we are facing a serious threat to national security. This epidemic, some are calling a plague, I prefer epidemic, is serious and very contagious. We are unclear at this time how it is being transmitted, but evidence is pointing to bodily fluids as the medium. Medical experts tell me that there is no known cure as of yet and that people should stay in their homes. While the mortality rate is near 90%, we are confident…"

He was interrupted by one of the reporters in the front row as he collapsed to the floor in a fit of coughing. Immediately there were cries of panic as people stepped back from the heavyset man from News Week, as others fled the room.

The camera man lost focus on the Governor and zoomed into the man on the floor. He was coughing continuously and seemed to be having trouble catching his breath. His nose started bleeding into his handkerchief and his eyes were quite red. A squad of security men in suits grabbed the Governor and led him off the stage. A team of men in Hazmat suits came in and carried the poor man out of the room.

Amid crying and confusion the rest of the newsmen and women, the camera men and sound men, all left the room. The camera went dark.

"OK. Well, ahem, this is Melody Manson reporting from Hartford, Connecticut where Governor Hansen has just been rushed from the Capital building as somebody in the room seemed to have a coughing spell right on camera. I hope he's OK. We'll keep you informed as long as we can. Oh. It's starting to rain again! Which reminds me! Stay tuned to this channel for local weather."

The camera shook from left to right which made Melody look like she was in an earthquake. She walked towards the camera.

"Chet are you OK? Are you sure? You don't... Oh no! Chet! Your nose is bleeding!"

The camera went dark.

Frank switched channels.

"...no known cure. CDC contagious disease director Melinda Chase said that they have identified the virus and are working to find something to fight it with."

The camera switched to a picture of Melinda.

"The virus was first discovered in a victim in Seattle, we're calling patient zero. The virus is not following normal dispersal patterns, so we are at a loss as to how it is spreading so fast. It would normally take weeks to travel across the continental United States. This virus is hitting in most countries in the world at the same time, or at least within hours. We have our best people working on this."

Sam and Rhonda could be seen behind her. They glanced at one another as a voice off camera asked "Ms Chase, what can people do to NOT get infected?"

Melinda, for the first time looked unsure of herself. She looked down at her notes and cleared her throat. When she looked up again, she looked angry.

"We know this can spread through bodily fluids. People should go to their homes and stay there until a cure is found. Avoid contact with others as much as possible. This virus can be beaten! I will not stop until a cure is found! I give you my word! Thank you."

Melinda turned and left the circle of microphones outside the CDC in Atlanta, where the sun was still shining.

Frank flipped channels and stopped on CNN.

"Washington State troops were deployed in Seattle after bodies were littering the streets. Soldiers in chemical warfare suits carrying automatic weapons are patrolling the streets. With martial law declared, now that night has fallen, if the plague doesn't get you the soldiers will. Several looters have been shot already today. John?"

"Thanks Sean. So, as we've heard today from around the world and now at home. Martial law has been declared nation-wide. Please folks, stay in your homes. If you have to go out for supplies, wait until morning and proceed with caution."

The phone rang. Frank picked it up.

"NOC, Frank here."

"Frank, it's Melinda, are you OK?" Melinda asked.

"Yes I'm fine. Are you OK?"

"Yes I'm fine. Frank, you need to get your family from home and take them to your work. It's the safest place right now." Melinda said urgently.

"Why Melinda? I was just going to go to them. It'll be dark soon."

"We've just received an email from a Dr. Novoas in Chile. He says that the virus is water-borne. Frank, it's in the clouds! That's how it's being dispersed so quickly! Stay out of the rain and don't drink the tap water, only bottled water. Chlorination does nothing. Boiling water does nothing. I've just notified the media. Please Frank just get your family to the office." Melinda pleaded.

"Why the office?" Frank asked.

"Is it still a filtered air environment?"

"Yes, but if it's water borne what difference does that make."

"Frank, this virus survives evaporation. Once it's dried, it becomes light as dust and can be spread by the wind. Air filtration should stop it."

"That's not like any virus I've ever heard of. It sounds like a prion carrier like mad cow disease."

"Very good Frank. You always were the smarter sibling! That's right. This is 'like' a prion, and 'like' a virus. It's a mutation we've never seen before. In fact, it doesn't look like anything on earth."

"Alien? You're kidding! Come on Melinda, an alien attack?"

"No Frank not an attack, it's a purely random occurrence. Remember the meteor threat? We think that it may have carried the virus. We are trying to get Fred Schoefield on the phone to see if he can show us where the meteor fragments went, but he's not answering."

"Who's that?"

"He's the one that alerted the world to the threat of the meteor. He's in Chile."

"OK. So bring my family here before dark?"

"Yes, and be careful. Hey! Pick up as much bottled water as you can. People will get desperate when the news breaks."

"OK. Thanks Melinda. I'll keep you in my prayers."

"Yeah, I'll need some of that. Thanks. Bye."

"Bye Melinda."

Frank called his wife.

"Honey? Pack up the kids we're going on a trip!"

"Where Frank? What are you talking about?"

"Honey, just be prepared to leave when I get home. There is a nasty flu epidemic going on and we'll be safest here at work."

"Flu? OK Frank, I'll be ready."

"Thanks Honey, I love you."

"I love you too! Bye."

Frank was thankful for a trusting wife. Many women would have wanted all the whys and wherefores. Not Julia. She was a peach.

Joan approached Frank from the work room.

"Hey Frank. What's going on?" she asked.

"Can you get your family here?" Frank said urgently.

"I guess so, why?" she asked

"I know this is hard to believe and I can't believe I'm saying this, but there is an alien virus raining down on us from the clouds, infecting and killing everyone it touches. Martial law has been declared and our homes are not safe. Please, Joan, trust me! Just get your family here!" Frank yelled, louder than he intended.

"OK, Frank. Jeez, calm down. Alien viruses? Are you sure?" Joan said in disbelief.

"Yes, Joan, I'm sure. I just spoke to my sister at the CDC, remember Melinda?" she nodded. "She just told me. Now move!"

"OK Frank!" Joan said as she ran to call her husband.

Frank grabbed his keys and his phone and ran towards the exit. After passing through the airlock and the security system Frank walked to his car. When he clicked the remote on his key fob, his car beeped twice to let him know it was unlocked. Frank looked around. People seemed to be carrying on with life as usual. There were people sitting at the Starbucks across the street laughing and talking about who knows what. People were walking up and down the street with their usual gate, eyes straight ahead, somewhere important to go. "Strange" Frank thought. "I guess I wasn't the last one to know!"

Frank got into his Mercedes and headed for home. On his way he stopped at Walmart and picked up two full carts of bottled water. There was a lineup as usual and only one cashier open. Frank went to the self-check-out and was soon out the door and to his car.

After filling the trunk and all available seats with bottled water, he drove the rest of the way home.

Chapter 22

The house was quiet except for the rain that was falling on the roof and overflowing the eves that were filled with pine needles and couldn't handle the heavy down poor. There was also inside the house the chorus of snores that competed with each other for dominance. Thirteen men in the four bedroom home were sound asleep.

The party had lasted until late at night and 4:30 came early, even for John Reed. His watch alarm went off for only one beep, before he turned it off. In fact he was already awake just seconds before and was waiting for it to go off, his finger poised over the watches button.

John rose and walked to his on suite bathroom, turned on his radio which was tuned to the oldies, relieved himself and dry toweled his face and hair, as was his custom. He'd shower and shave and brush his teeth after his run.

One wall of his bathroom contained bookshelves filled with rolled tee shirts, socks and folded shorts. In one corner was a cedar lined and covered laundry hamper where used jogging outfits were tossed. John selected a set of clothes and changed into them ready for his run.

On the radio, the music that had been playing stopped suddenly and an announcer came on the air.

"Breaking News from your oldies station KKING, the flu virus that hit our city yesterday has been designated as an epidemic by the CDC. Melinda Chase Director of

the Infectious Disease Division released a statement today that the virus is water borne and lethal within 24 hours.

In other words, it is in the drinking water, and in the rain that's falling on us right now! Don't drink the water and stay out of the rain!

Washington State troops have been deployed in downtown Seattle after bodies were found littering the streets. Soldiers in chemical warfare suits carrying automatic weapons are patrolling the streets. With martial law declared, now that night has fallen, if the plague doesn't get you the soldiers will. Several looters have been shot already.

Martial law has been declared nation-wide. Please folks, stay in your homes. If you have to go out for supplies, wait until morning and proceed with caution."

John turned off the radio and looked out his bathroom window. The falling rain was still invisible as the sun had not yet come up, but he could see droplets hitting the window.

John's mind raced. He was already considering the many scenarios that could play out and what his response should be. He could easily lock down his house with the men he currently had. They had reasonable protection from the rain in their jungle gear. He had the means to survive for several weeks with the supplies in his barn. He also had some large tents that could house a few people. The question on his mind was does he just protect himself and his men, or does he help those in the community that need it. John's life had been one of service to his country and the question was easily decided in favor of the community. He would help who he could.

John decided the fastest way to get his groggy and hung over men awake was to instigate a knee-jerk response. John turned on all the lights and set off the house alarm.

Each of the men were instantly awake and on their feet weapons at the ready, looking for a threat. Finding none, they grumbled and complained. "What's going on!" said some, "Who's the idiot!?", and others just mumbled obscenities and tried to find their pillow again.

"Gentlemen, fall in!" Lieutenant Colonel John Reed said using his command voice.

Recognizing the seriousness and timbre of their commander's voice they formed two rows and stood at attention, listening intently.

"We have a situation. I don't know if any of you have heard the news of the flu epidemic that has hit Seattle?" John began, looking around. Some nodded others looked at John questioningly.

"Well it is serious. Apparently martial law has been declared in Seattle, and night curfews are in place. This virus is incredibly contagious, virulent and is water born. Do you remember the Bilharzia we encountered in South Africa? Well this virus is water born as well except this virus is fatal. It's in the rain and the drinking water so only hydrate from bottled water." John finished.

"What's the plan Colonel?" asked Connie.

"We are going to set up a refuge here and help as many people as we can. If you go outside wear your rain gear. Don't let the water into your eyes nose or mouth. I have supplies, but we'll need more. We'll need to set up a defensive perimeter to keep out stupid idiots that want to steal our supplies. We have tents to set up and we'll need latrines dug. Use anything I have to get the job done. Any questions?" John asked.

"How do you want to handle intruders?" Connie asked.

"Force to force." John answered. They all knew what he meant as the UN used a similar policy. Fire when fired upon, gun for gun, knife for knife, hand to hand, they were to respond in kind.

"What about quarantine?" asked another of the men with medical training.

"Good idea Tim." John answered. "Let's make one of the tents a quarantine for new people brought in. 24 hour quarantine. Initially though, anyone showing symptoms will not be allowed in. Tim, you take care of that." Tim nodded his head once in acknowledgement.

"Let's get to it!" John commanded.

John pulled out a map of his property and laid it on the kitchen table. Several of the men gathered around while others got dressed and headed outside and got right to work moving vehicles, closing the gate, and patrolling the perimeter.

John mapped out where the tents, latrines and supplies could go. They formed teams and the men dispersed. John and Connie and a couple of other men remained behind.

"I'll take inventory and take a ride into town and have a looksee. I'll take Moore and Jones wi'me, they're good lads. Shall I take the Humvee?" Connie asked.

"You might as well, who knows what it's like out there? Be prepared and be careful. After all these years I'd hate to lose you to a bug." John said sincerely.

"It'll take more than that to kill Cornelius Patrick Quinn Boyo!" said Connie with a laugh.

"All the same…" John reiterated.

"All righty, I'll be careful!" Connie agreed. He turned smartly and said to Moore and Jones, "C'mon lads, let's go shopping!"

"Yessir!" they said in unison and followed him out the door, grabbing their gear as they went.

John looked again at the map on the table. He could defend himself adequately from below, but Cougar Mountain at his back was problematic. Someone could fire on him from above and have the advantage. He'd have to set up patrols through the woods and lay some defensive hardware to keep out intruders. He looked out the window and saw his men already at work in the rain. John took a deep breath and blew it out in a sigh. "Here we go again." he said to himself, and went to work.

Chapter 23

"It's impossible! How can a living thing be impervious to every test designed to kill it?" Jacob Wettstien asked. He was addressing the team in Melinda's office. Noah Drew had completed his testing, Sam Smith and Rhonda Lewis had completed their calculations and Melinda Chase had been in touch with every world health representative.

"The only explanation is that it is not of this world. It seems not to be a carbon based life form. More like some kind of silicon. In its inert state, it appears to be nothing more than a spec of microscopic dust. But when it gets wet it comes to life." Noah explained to the team.

"Have you tried radiation or extreme heat?" asked Jacob.

"Yes, and to no avail. When exposed to high doses of radiation, the virus seems to shrink in size and become harder. The barbs it uses for attaching to human tissue retreat and it becomes a simple sphere." Noah answered.

"Could it then be flushed from the victim using a radical blood transfusion?" asked Melinda.

"No, I'm afraid not Melinda. I thought of that, but the dose of radiation required to effect the virus would kill the patient.

Even extreme heat cannot kill the virus. It seems to have the properties of a prion, as you suggested Melinda, but it is so much larger than one. When blasted with 3000°F it simply shrinks in size, pulls in its barbs and goes inert. As soon as it encounters moisture, it comes back to life. Obviously, that kind of heat would kill the patient too." Noah replied.

"I have tried everything I could think of. I am open to suggestions, even wild ones." said Noah.

Melinda took charge again.

"OK. We will not give up on this. The mortality rate is 100% folks! We know it is water borne thanks to Dr. Novoas in Chile, but how did it get into the water? Where did it come from?"

"Well, we know that India was the first to report a new virus at work in the flooding there." Sam said as he pulled up the holographic globe.

The globe rotated showing a red line all across Canada, and half way down the United States. There was a gap in the Southern states all the way to Florida, but another red line started again south of the equator. The width of the line was greater on the Pacific coast and lesser on the Eastern Seaboard.

Northern Europe was just starting to show red, but starting in India Eastward it was already a wide band.

"The pattern looked familiar to me, but I couldn't quite figure it out. Rhonda suggested the jet stream."

Rhonda blushed.

"As you can see, when I superimpose the jet streams over the world map it is very close. Obviously the

Jetstream is constantly moving and changing with the Earths Coriolis effect, and when I adjust for time passing…."

The map changed and the two graphics overlapped perfectly, although the thicknesses of the bands were different.

"If I also reverse the process so that the jet stream and the virus spread are in time synchronization, you can see that the red spots begin over the north and south Pacific Oceans and the Indian Ocean." Sam sat back and waited for any questions.

"Good job Sam, this confirms my suspicions." said Melinda.

"What suspicion?" asked Jacob.

"My suspicion is that this virus came from the meteor." Melinda said quite seriously.

"Come on Melinda. You are grasping at straws. That's completely ridiculous. There has never before been any proof that life exists anywhere but on earth. This is probably the work of man's ego. Someone thought they could design a better virus to use as a weapon. The Iraqis are obviously responsible and they have responded to the nuclear attack by our war-mongering, arrogant United States President with a biological weapon of mass destruction." Jacob concluded.

Melinda leaned forward. "Jacob, I respect your opinion." She said sincerely. "but we do not have the capability anywhere on this planet to design a silicon based life form. One that seems to have basic intelligence and responds to stimuli in a way that is unlike anything else we've encountered. We have seen before what man can come up with. The weapon used by the Iraqis against US troops was deadly, but it was simple by comparison to this virus."

She paused in thought.

"I would like to continue trying to contact Frederick Schoefield in Chile. I hope he can give us the telemetry of the meteor as it broke up in the atmosphere. Remember that it was made of ice. That could easily have carried an alien virus into our world."

"Yes, but it burned up in the atmosphere during reentry. Nothing hit the ground!" Jacob stated smugly.

"That is true Jacob. However, Noah's testing indicated that it could survive the heat of reentry. I'd like Sam to continue trying to contact the Paranal Observatory to confirm my suspicion."

"No problem Melinda." said Sam.

"Rhonda, have you calculated the rate of spread?" asked Melinda.

"Yes I have." Rhonda replied.

The globe changed and turned as the red spread over the whole world in a matter of seconds. Jacob dropped his pencil took of his glasses and swore under his breath. Noah grabbed his head as if to squeeze out the horror he was seeing. Sam swallowed hard. Rhonda's lips quivered and she held onto Sam's hand.

Melinda asked "How long do we have Rhonda? What was the timeframe for world coverage?"

Rhonda cleared her throat. "Well, it's not a perfect algorithm. But I'm pretty sure that we have less than a week before the whole world is infected."

"This is a doomsday virus. With no cure, this is a world killer." Noah said what everyone else was thinking.

"Not my world!" Melinda said angrily. "We will not give up hope. Now do your jobs, the world is depending on us!"

The team stood as one. Each of them nodded and walked out of her office. Melinda picked up the phone and dialed her daughter's cell phone. On the fifth ring Jessica picked up the phone.

"What do you want Mom?"

"Hi Jess!   Could you do me a favor?" asked Melinda.

"No, I'm with friends right now. Can't it wait, whatever it is?" Jessica said impatiently.

"Jess, I need you to listen to me. There is a viral epidemic coming and it's spread by water. Stay out of the rain, and drink only bottled water. I need you to come to work and stay with me for a while."

"You've got a weird sense of humor Mom. Is this some kind of CDC joke? It's not funny."

"No Jessica Diane Chase, I am not joking! You get your…" Melinda gained control of herself. "Would you please come here as soon as you can, no joke."

"You are serious, aren't you?" said Jessica.

"Dead serious Jessica."

"What about Daddy?"

Melinda thought of her estranged husband. He *had* left her.

"Mom?!"

"OK, Jess you can bring him too."

"OK. I'll see you in a while. Thanks Mom!"

"I love you Jess!" Melinda said too late after they had already been disconnected.

Melinda stood up from her desk and turned to look out the window. Downtown Atlanta was lit up beautifully as usual this night. She could see her reflection in the window and after a few moments the woman in the window started to cry. Tears of frustration ran down her cheeks as she took a steadying breath and wiped her eyes with a Kleenex from her pocket.

For the first time in her life she was faced with failure. Never before had she been defeated by a virus, disease or bacteria. She didn't like the feeling much.

She dried her eyes and took another deep breath, letting it out slowly. Squaring her shoulders and pocketing the Kleenex, and turned from the window.

As she turned, lightening flashed, followed by a thunderous roar. It made Melinda jump. She turned back to the window as large drops of rain began to pelt her office window making sparkling rivulets of water on the outside.

"So it begins." Melinda said to no one in particular.

Chapter 24

The Space Needle was reflected brightly in the puddle formed in the street. A black boot stepped through the puddle leaving the Space Needle warped and wavering.

The rain was falling in sheets as the soldiers formed an impenetrable wall that marched toward the crowd gathered on Broad Street in Seattle, Washington. The drenched crowd, made up of hundreds men women and children, old and young had gathered in protest, demanding action against the 'flu' epidemic that had killed thousands of people.

The solders held riot shields and M16s. They were wearing black glistening rainwear, chemical warfare masks and gloves. Their helmets had clear visors under which could be seen the goggles of their mask and the round breathing apparatus of the air filtration system. Looking like a row of Darth Vader clones, they marched in step closer to the protestors.

A voice boomed from a loudspeaker atop a Humvee.

"Go to your homes. The President has declared martial law. You are past curfew and must evacuate this area. You are in danger. Leave immediately or you will be fired upon."

"What are you going to do? Kill us? We're dead already!" yelled one man.

"Give us medicine! My daughter is sick!" cried one young woman holding her coughing child.

A young lieutenant was standing beside the Humvee. He had his mask in one hand and a microphone in the other. He had desperation in his voice when he pleaded. "Please! Please! For God's sake, leave the area and return to your homes!"

"We need medicine! We need a cure! Where is FEMA? Where is the Mayor?" asked another with a bullhorn.

The crowd raised their fists defiantly beginning again a chorus of shouting and began to throw bottles and trash at the soldiers.

The lieutenant order the soldier manning the 50 caliber mounted to the Humvee to fire a few rounds above the crowds head.

It had the desired effect on many in the crowd. Several dozen of them ducked and ran away from the gunfire. Others however became angrier and after the initial shock of the gunfire, charged the riot line. Some of them carrying weapons opened fire on the troops.

When one of the soldiers went down, and at the command of the lieutenant, the 50 caliber machine gun opened fire on the crowd. The riot line pulled back to avoid the spray of deadly gunfire and pulled the wounded solder behind the line.

The protestors were not so lucky. A 50 caliber bullet will devastate a human body. A direct hit to the torso will cut someone in half. A bullet to the shoulder or hip will sever the whole arm or leg. A hit to the head and there would be nothing left recognizable.

When the machine gun stopped firing, there was complete silence except for the sound of the rain, and the sound of the gun barrel as it crackled and hissed as it cooled. There was though another, awful sound. It was the groaning and the cries of the poor souls who were not quite dead.

Several soldiers doubled over and opening their masks, vomited on the sodden ground.

There was a sudden report from behind the soldiers who turned to see where the danger was. What they saw was the young lieutenant - face down on the ground with his own smoking gun in his hand. Blood from the bullet wound in his head mixed with the blood of the protestors and with the rain that continued to pour down from the darkening sky.

Chapter 25

The California Highway Patrol car drove casually through the Redwood Regional Park on Skyline Boulevard, Oakland, California. Officer Chappy Inez had slowed down because of the poor visibility. It was raining heavily and his car's windshield wipers were frantically trying to keep up with the pouring rain.

Through the darkness ahead he saw an animal walk into the glow of his headlights. However, as he skidded to a stop and turned on his high-beams, he realized that it wasn't an animal but a man on all fours, crawling onto the road.

The officer turned on the red and blue emergency lights and trained his spotlight on the man. He put on his hat and slipped on his slicker and exited the patrol car. Then he grabbed his flashlight and walked towards the man. Officer Inez suspected a drunkard, but he didn't see a car on the shoulder anywhere ahead.

One hand on his gun and the other holding the flashlight he approached the man on the road.

"Hey mister!" there was no response.

"Hey mister! Police! Don't move!" Officer Inez commanded.

"Help me!" was the response of the man.

Now that he was closer Officer Inez saw that the man was wearing a dark suit and tie and sun glasses. As he approached the man sat down on the road and held his hands out to show he had no weapons.

"Help me!" the man said again.

Officer Inez cautiously walked forward and stooped to look at the man's face.

"Are you alright Mister?" he asked.

The man started to cough violently.

"Hey! Take it easy!" said the officer stepping back he thought of the plague he had heard about on the news. Maybe this guy has it! He thought to himself. "You stay here, I'll get you some help" he said. As he turned around there was another man in a dark suit behind him. "Hi!" the man said, and punched Officer Inez in the face, knocking the officer out cold.

"Let's go Bobby! Good decoy!" He pocketed the gun from the holster of Officer Inez and dragged him to the side of the road.

"Let's go Bobby! Hurry up!" he said again.

Bobby got up slowly and staggered towards the car entering the passenger seat. "I don't feel too good Jim" he said as he started coughing again.

"You've picked up a bug or something. Don't worry about it, you'll feel better once we get to that feisty Matthew Parker's house. We owe him one don't you think?"

"Sure Jim, sure." Bobby said breathing heavily.

As they pulled away and drove off into the night, neither Bobby nor Jim, the mercenary twins, knew how close they were to their own death.

Officer Chappy Inez lay slept face up on the grass. The rain pouring on his face easily flowed into his open mouth as he lay there helplessly.

Chapter 26

Derek Manheim sat at his desk in the computer lab. He had searched the entire facility and found nothing but dead bodies. Each and every one he found had the same grotesque look and had died the same way; gasping for breath and coughing uncontrollably. Derek had gathered all the bottled water he could find in all the vending machines, and in the cafeteria. He had about seventy half liter bottles and by his estimates he could survive about two weeks. After that he'd have to try to survive on milk, sodas and energy drinks which would give him another few days. If no help arrived he'd have to leave the facility and search for food and water and any help he could find.

Derek placed his head in his hands, and sighed. "I can't believe that I am the only one left." He said.

"You are not alone Derek!" said KAMY the Artificial Intelligence computer.

"Thanks KAMY. I know you are still there. But you can't exactly help me now." Derek stated sadly.

"I do have something to tell you though Derek." said KAMY

"What's that KAMY?" Derek asked.

"I have been monitoring the phone system and someone has been trying to reach Dr. Schoefield several dozen times."

"How do you know that? The telephone system is not part of your systems." Derek asked.

"No it isn't Derek, but we are friends." I have the voice messages if you want to hear them. Maybe help is available after all." replied KAMY.

"That's cool KAMY. Play it back please."

"Playing… "

The voice message could be heard through the speakers.

"Dr. Schoefield, this is Melinda Chase from the CDC. I was hoping to reach you regarding the breakup of the meteors and the trajectory of the pieces. We believe that the world wide pandemic is being caused by a virus contained in the ice and spread by the jet stream. We would like to confirm this. If you would please call me back at 1-800-CDC-INFO extension 433. Thank you!"

"KAMY I don't know if you can, but can you dial her back?" asked Derek hopefully.

"It would be my pleasure Derek."

The phone's dial tone could be heard through the speakers, followed by the tones of the number being dialed. After a few rings, the phone in Atlanta was picked up.

"Welcome to the CDC. If you know the extension of the party you are calling enter it now."

KAMY entered the extension and the phone rang again.

"Melinda Chase"

"Melinda, this is Derek Manheim calling from Paranal, Chile. You were trying to contact Dr. Frederick Schoefield regarding the meteor's trajectory." Derek said.

"Yes, Derek, thanks for calling me back. How's it there?" asked Melinda.

"It's pretty bad, Melinda. I am the only one left alive. Everyone is dead." His voice cracked as he answered.

"I'm so sorry Derek. I'm afraid the news is similar all around the world. The mortality rate is 100% for those infected and many are dead or infected in every city in the world. Only those in the arid areas of the world have been unaffected. You see, the virus we suspect has come in from another world, carried by the meteor. When the meteor split into pieces, the virus was disbursed by the jet stream. At least that is our theory. Can you provide us with your data on the trajectory of the meteor's pieces?"

"That is simple, please provide your email address Melinda." said KAMY.

"Who is that Derek, I thought you were alone?" asked Melinda.

"I am alone. That is KAMY my AI computer. She has a voice interface that interacts with me, you, us." Derek explained.

"Well, hello KAMY. My email address is MChase@cdc.gov."

"Thank you Melinda, pleased to make your acquaintance. Computing…" there was a pause and then KAMY concluded.

"Transmission completed."

"Wow! It would be nice to have an AI computer like you at the CDC, KAMY. Ever consider a career change?" asked Melinda.

"I am afraid I'm not a mobile computer Melinda. But thanks for the offer." said KAMY.

"I hate to break it up girls, but what am I supposed to do now?" asked Derek

"Derek, your data will help us fight this horrible virus. We are in your debt. If I have any influence at all in what is left of our military, I will try and send help. Hang in there for a few days." said Melinda.

"That would be great Melinda. I only have two weeks of water left, and barely enough food to last that long. If help doesn't arrive by then, I'll have to set out on my own."

"Let's pray that doesn't happen. Your chances of avoiding the virus outside of a closed facility are pretty slim. Remember that the virus is water borne. That means it's in the rain, the reservoirs, the lakes, the rivers and the oceans. It will be in puddles, in drains and anywhere else where there is standing water. We haven't confirmed this yet, but we are predicting that mosquitoes will be carriers of the virus, so you should use lots of deet repellent as well." said Melinda.

"Well, I sure hope you get here then! Anything else you need?"

"No, I've just received the data. Thank you so much for your help!"

"I've got nothing else to do. I mean, you are welcome!"

"OK, Derek. Thanks again!" Melinda said as she hung up.

"Well, KAMY, it's just you and me now." said Derek.

"Derek, we will make it through. Please be aware that the lab door is ajar. Please close it to keep the mosquitoes out." KAMY suggested.

"OK. Thanks for the warning." Derek said as he went over and closed the door. "KAMY, can you connect to any computer system?" he asked.

"Yes I can."

"Great, how about some music? Can you hook into my computer and access the playlist?" he asked.

Latin music began to play over the speakers. It was a joyful rhythm with an orchestra and brass cheerfully sending notes throughout the lab. Derek walked over to the couch in the corner of the lab and lay down on it. He was soon fast asleep.

The rain continued to fall on the mountains of Chile. Antofagasta was a ghost town littered with the bodies of those that succumbed to the Manheim Virus. Traffic was not moving, deserted cars littered the roadways and an ambulance, it's lights still flashing, it's siren still going, had come to rest against the emergency entrance doors to the Hospital. The EMT was laying on the steering wheel, his partner and a patient wearing a business suit, were in the back. The patient's name tag read, Dr. Enrique Novoas. All were dead. Victims of the alien virus.

Chapter 27

Frank Chase was concerned as he arrived in his driveway. His front door was open, as was the garage door. Household items were strewn all over the yard but no one was in sight.

Frank got out of his car and walked cautiously towards his open front door. He saw his son's baseball bat on the ground and he picked it up and entered through the front door.

"Honey? You here?" he called out.

The house was a mess. It was as if a tornado had ripped through the house and picked up everything inside and threw it against the walls.

"Julia!" Frank called again.

He walked through the entire house and found no one. The only place left was the basement. It was down the stairs through the door in the kitchen. The door was closed and locked from the inside. He listened with his ear to the door and he heard a faint crying. He knocked.

"Honey?!" he called out. "Are you there?"

"Frank!" Julia cried. "Daddy!" Samantha called out excitedly. The other children joined in a chorus of "Daddy!"

The door lock rattled and the door flew open. His wife and children were on the stairs trying to get out and hug their Daddy.

"I'm so glad you're here! I was so scared Frank." said Julia.

"What happened?" asked Frank.

"They came in through the garage door. It was open because little Frank left it open after he'd taken out the garbage."

"Who were they?"

"They were a bunch of guys, I don't know. I didn't recognize any of them. They came in and just started taking things. The TV, the stereo, even food from the cupboards and the fridge! Frank, they threatened us and told us to leave; to leave our own house Frank!" Julia sobbed.

"It's OK Honey, it's just stuff. We do need to go though - now." Frank said.

"But Frank. What about our house? We should call the police!" she said.

"Julia, they are too busy. The city is a mess. People are going crazy with this virus. It's very dangerous. Get what you can together for you and the kids. We need to get to the office before dark, there's a curfew in place." Frank looked outside. The sun was already on the horizon. Frank gave Julia a hug. "Come on Honey, we have to go!"

Julia started picking up things off the floor and ordering the children about. With everyone helping they were out the door in five minutes. Frank had transferred the bottled water from his Mercedes to the Chrysler Minivan while the others were getting things together. As the last one was buckled in, Frank went back into the house. In the living room above the bookshelf he reached his shotgun and shells. Fortunately, the looters didn't find it.

As Frank got into the car, Julia saw the shotgun. "Do you think we'll need that?" she asked.

"I hope not Julia. It's better to have it though, just in case." Frank answered.

Frank backed out of the driveway and headed for CTTEL. He switched on his lights and his wipers as it had just started to rain.

"Oh Frank! Didn't you say the virus is in the rain?" asked Julia.

"I did. We'll be OK. I'll use the underground parking, we won't even get wet." He said trying to allay his wife's fears.

As they drove through Branford Harbor many of the houses were being looted. People were fighting with each other and flashes of gunfire could be seen. People were running in all directions. Frank had to swerve several times to avoid hitting people. Some were loading vehicles with food and water trying to get out of town. Others were loading vehicles with TVs and stereos, computers and furniture, trying to steal the good stuff before someone else did. Several were on the ground bleeding, others were motionless.

The rain became a shower as they left the town and got onto highway 95. Traffic was heavy but moving. Most of the traffic seemed to be heading out of Hartford, not into it so they made good progress. Still it took them more than an hour to get to the exit they wanted and then traffic came to a standstill. Exit 32B off 91 took them onto Trumbull street, but before they got to Chapel Street a road block had been set up.

Through his rain streaked windshield Frank couldn't see any police lights, or any State Troopers. He didn't see military vehicles, but did see some in camouflage outfits, and several holding guns, others holding bright flashlights.

Frank grew suspicious as he drew closer. Several cars were on the side of the road and the contents spilled on the ground. At the car in front of him a man was pulled out and thrown to the ground. His wife was pulled out the other side and thrown down also. Two men got into the car drove the it through the barricade and off to the left with many other cars. The men got out and started hauling bottled water out of the car and into a box truck.

Knowing what was about to happen to him, Frank told the children to get down in the back seats. "Julia, get down too!"

"Frank!" she said with a quivering whisper.

"Trust me Julia, it'll be OK." Frank said with a smile.

Frank put a round into the chamber of the shotgun and lay it on his lap at the ready. He pulled up to the barricade.

"Good evening Sir. Please step out of the vehicle." said a man dressed in fatigues.

"Is there a problem?" asked Frank.

"Do you know there is a curfew Sir? You are in violation of that curfew. Martial Law is in effect. Step out of the vehicle Sir!"

"Let me see some ID!" demanded Frank.

"Sir, If you don't step out of the vehicle you will be forcibly removed!"

"I don't think so!" Frank raised the shotgun and pointed it at the man's face. "Move aside!" he commanded.

The man took a step back. Frank used the moment to step on the gas and the minivan pushed forward through the barricade. As Frank raced away, flashes of gunfire could be seen in his side mirrors, and ricochets sparked off the metal of the car. The rear window was broken as a bullet passed through the vehicle and hit the dash between Frank and Julia. Frank swerved from side to side and put some distance between them and the barricade. They were soon the few blocks to the CTTEL building.

Frank pulled into the entrance to the underground parking and pulled up to the closed gate. The gate had already been closed for the night and had the security fence down. When Frank pushed his id card into the gate key, the fence went up and the barricade rose, allowing them to pass. As they went through the gate it began to close again.

Frank pulled up in a spot close to the elevator.

"OK. Everyone out! Let's go!" Frank commanded.

Julia and the children each grabbed something and they headed to the elevator. After a few trips they were safely inside with all their supplies.

Joan and her family were already there and greetings were exchanged.

"Joan, did anyone else come in?" asked Frank in a concerned voice.

"I'm afraid not. I tried everyone, but no one answered. It's just us Frank. I'm sorry." said Joan sadly.

"It's OK Joan. I know you tried." said Frank.

"Alright folks. Let's get organized, take an inventory and then we'll see what's going on on the TV." Frank suggested.

They all busied themselves with sorting and stacking water, food, and supplies and Frank took notes on a clipboard. After a few minutes they were done.

"Good job everyone. I'm going to secure the building. You all stay here." Frank said as he left the NOC.

Frank walked through the facility and checked all the doors. He locked down all the security terminals and disabled the card entry systems.

Frank went to the twelfth floor and looked out the window. From this viewpoint he could see the lights of police cars going through the city. Fires could be seen as buildings burned freely. Fire trucks went by on their way to help, but there were more fires than they could possibly handle.

The rain continued to pour down from the night sky. The city was still brightly lit, but belayed the feeling of helplessness Frank felt. The virus was winning. In the terror of that thought, Frank reflected on the inherent evil in man.

Many thought that man was inherently good, and through bad circumstances and a poor upbringing man could be made bad. But Frank believed the Bible, which said that man is born in sin and does good only when he is enabled of God to do so. "If we ever needed saving, now is the time. Please God, help us!" Frank said out loud.

Chapter 28

Dr. Thomas Katz stood behind a curtain examining another victim of the epidemic. Nurse Nixon was on the other side of the patient's bed.

"Nurse, have you sedated this patient?" he asked through the surgical mask.

"Yes Doctor, as you requested." Nurse Nixon replied, also wearing a mask.

"This sedation is having no affect. Give him 100mg more intravenously" Dr. Katz ordered.

Nurse Nixon, wearing surgical gloves, injected the sedative into the IV port. Immediately there was a response. The patient, Louis Vegaz, a 40 year old obese man started to spasm and twist, his eyes bulged and the blood vessels burst in his eyes. He started to cough again and the straps they had secured him with earlier strained to hold him.

"Nurse, hold him!" Dr. Katz demanded.

As they held him down the coughing ended suddenly. Dr. Katz was desperate to save this man.

"Nurse prepare to intubate him. Quickly!"

Nurse Nixon lifted the two piece device from the tray beside her, and handed it to Dr. Katz.

Dr. Katz wearing his own gloves tilted the patients head back in an attempt to insert the metal depressor and push the tongue down. He couldn't even do that. Even as he tried the tongue was continuing to swell. He swore under his breath and tried harder.

"Doctor!" Nurse Nixon touched the doctor's shoulder to get his attention. "It's no use. He's just like the others."

Thomas threw the device against the wall in anger. "Then what am I supposed to do! I am a Doctor! I save lives! I am helpless against this virus!"

"Comfort and contain, your words doctor." Nurse Nixon said softly. She had seen enough death to last a lifetime in the last 36 hours.

As they stepped side by side out from behind the curtain they could see the hallway in both directions was filled with hospital gurneys. Each one contained from two to four bodies stacked on top of each other covered in bloody sheets. There were people in the waiting areas, not a seat vacant. Some were dead where they sat; others sat staring motionlessly into space.

The hospital had long ago locked its doors. Crowds of people were gathered outside the double doors of the Emergency room demanding help, desperate to help their loved ones, or themselves.

The police had also been overwhelmed and called back. All that stood between the crowds and those inside were two glass doors and a nervous security guard.

Eric O'Neal had retired six years ago from the Seattle Police Department. In thirty years of service he'd never had to fire his gun at a real target. He was in administration, pushing paper, keeping the police department supplied with everything they needed from paper clips to rocket launchers.

As the crowd outside grew wilder, he yelled for them to stay back. He drew his gun and held it aloft as a warning. This enraged the crowd and the looked for a way to break down the doors. One of them picked up a cement garbage can holder and threw it at the doors. The glass doors shattered and the crowd poured through. Those in front were quickly trampled as hundreds of people streamed in.

Some hopped over the admitting counter and went through the cabinets looking for medicine. Others took saline bags from patients already in ICU beds.

Security Guard Eric O'Neal fired in the air. Everyone stopped moving. All eyes turned on him. "Now listen to me!" he said with more authority than he felt. "We are going to try to help everyone, please form a line to my right and we'll take your names."

Before he could continue, a man dressed in leather, his back emblazoned with a flaming skull and the words "Pale Riders" hit Eric over the head with a rope stanchion and knocked him to the ground unconscious. Taking the security guard's gun he held it up and screamed "Yeah!" The crowd cheered with him, but were silenced again by Dr. Katz. Removing his mask he began to speak.

"Hey! I'm Dr. Thomas Katz, I'm in charge here. Look we don't want any trouble. Give me the gun and take a seat, and we'll do the best we can to see everyone." He said smoothly.

"No buddy, I'm in charge! I have the gun. Or didn't you notice, *Doctor*?"

"Yes, I noticed. But I am the only one that can help any of you. This violence is not help. If you want help, give me the gun, and let me see what I can do." Thomas said stepping forward with his hand out, hoping to appeal to common sense.

The biker pointed the gun at Thomas and fired without hesitation, then smiled and pocketed the revolver then turned and ran off to get his share.

Thomas was pushed back against the wall by the impact of the 38 bullet and slid down the wall leaving a brilliant stain of red as he went. The last thing he saw was the crowd running back and forth with pills, vials, bandages and packages in their hands.

Then before darkness overwhelmed his vision he saw Nurse Nixon's look of concern, felt the caress of her hand on his face as she said. "Oh Thomas, No…"

Chapter 29

"Hello?"

"Francis, it's Matt." said Matt as he entered Oakland California and made his way around Lake Merrit on his way to 7th St where the Oakland Police Department was located in the city's center.

"Matthew, what do you want?" asked Dr. Magee.

"Francis, they threatened me. They told me to stay away from the police or they'd kill me." said Matt urgently.

"I told you they were not to be messed with. What's that to me?" asked Dr. Magee.

"They said if I went to the police, they'd also hurt you and Monique. I don't really care what they do to you Magee, but I care for your wife and wouldn't want anything to happen to her."

"That's touching Matt, I didn't know you cared so much. I'll be sure to tell her of your concern." said Dr. Magee sarcastically.

"Look, Francis. The man I spoke with meant business; I barely escaped with my life. Please take care of Monique." pleaded Matt.

"She's packing right now Matthew, coincidentally, so am I. We are catching a plane to Arizona." Dr. Magee said.

"Why Arizona? What's there?" asked Matt.

"The virus isn't there yet Matthew. It's the only safe haven as of right now." Dr. Magee said.

"What are you talking about? What virus? If this is another one of your get-rich-quick schemes, I would think you'd be more worried about getting caught than that. I'm only blocks away from the police department." Matt asked.

"I don't care about the police Matthew, they'll all be dead soon anyway. Watch the news Matthew! Clear your head! Jennings is the least of my worries. Best of luck to you! For old time's sake old boy!" Dr. Magee said sincerely as he hung up the phone.

"Virus?" Matt said to himself. He turned on the radio.

"...stay out of the rain. The virus, called the Manheim virus after the meteor that carried it to our world, has been found everywhere around the world. Worldwide martial law is in effect. Do not go outside after dark, you will be arrested, detained or worse. Looters will be shot on site. Once again, do not go out in the rain, it contains the virus and is very contagious. Drink only bottled water. The Governor asks you to conserve your bottled water, as the virus is in the water supply."

The radio newsman continued to speak as Matthew pulled up half a block away from the Police Department.

Outside Matthew was astounded by what he saw. People were everywhere, running back and forth in the rain. Policemen and civilians were wrestling in front of the doors. One policeman with a bull horn spoke loudly to the crowd.

"Go to your homes! There is nothing we can do for you! Please, go to your homes! Go home and stay out of the rain!" he pleaded.

"We need water! There is none in the stores and tap water is contaminated! What are we supposed to do?" asked a women in the crowd.

"I don't know!" the policeman said. "Go home! Obey the curfew! The National Guard will be patrolling the streets and you need to be in your homes. Go Home!" The policeman's voice was overwhelmed by the yelling of the crowd, which seemed to gain strength as Matthew watched.

Matt pulled away from the curb and drove slowly away, avoiding attention. He had to find out more about this virus.

"An alien virus from outer space?" Matt thought to himself.

Matt pressed down on the gas pedal as he sped out of Oakland, onto the Nimitz freeway and headed for home.

Outside Matthew's home, in a police cruiser hidden in the trees were the mercenary twins. Bobby and Jim were waiting for Matthew to arrive. When he did they'd show him how they could fight when they weren't sucker punched.

Chapter 30

"Thanks Jacob." said Melinda Chase as she hung up the phone. Melinda was at her desk and had just spoken to Jacob Wettstein. Jacob had just finished telling Melinda what Red Callaghan had reported from the Whitehouse.

The U.S. military was being hit heavily. The National Guard was doing the best it could in the major cities, but small towns were on their own. Much of the military at home were ill equipped to handle biological agents and many thousands had been lost through faulty or nonexistent biological gear. Abroad the US soldiers feared better as they were prepared for chemical and biological attacks as a routine.

Atlanta was not immune to the effects of the virus. People had panicked and started looting and burning as soon as sign of infection had begun. An armored division and an infantry division from Fort Benning near Columbus had set up a four block perimeter around the CDC. They were as secure as they could hope for.

The nuclear attack against Iraq had been a success by military standards but it was now only a minor concern for the CDC in comparison to the pandemic caused by the Manheim Virus.

Some cities that had superior filtration in the water treatment facilities had success in filtering out some but not all of the Manheim Virus. They had claimed success, but it was short lived as people started to get sick from the water. Reportedly they had tried everything they could think of with no success.

FEMA had lost all credibility with the media and with the public. They were just incapable of coping with the scale of the disaster.

State and local governments had all but broken down and there was anarchy in the streets. As the days passed there was less and less violence though as there were less and less people to protest or riot. Soon Major cities became ghost towns.

Initially, cities like San Francisco and Los Angeles tried to deal with the bodies to stop the spread of the virus. Bulldozers scooped up bodies in the streets and stacked them in dump trucks.

These were carried to stadiums previously used for football games where the bodies were dumped and burned. Of course the burning had the opposite effect than was intended. Instead of containing the virus, it spread the virus as the stench of burning bodies rose with thick black clouds and carried the virus back up into the air where it mixed with the rain and poured back down on the helpless people of the city.

There was some good news, however. Fortress communes were formed by those not yet infected. These makeshift communities were ruled by ex-military men with courage and conscious. They used their leadership ability to form militia, set up defensive positions, and set up quasi-governments with civilian judges.

These communes were self-sustaining, and used search and rescue missions to gather water, food and bring in those people who were not yet infected. Those brought in were quarantined for 24 hours before they were allowed into the general population.

Ham radios were used for communication between communes and they exchanged useful information with each other.

New York City was quiet though. No one had heard anything from that city for days and the worst was assumed. The list went on. Portland, Provost, Billings, Chicago, and Pittsburg were silent.

Melinda's phone rang again. Her outside line hadn't stopped ringing for days. She had given up answering it. She stared at it unblinking as it rang again. She didn't know how long she had been like that when she was startled by John McKenzie.

"Melinda!" he said again.

"Sorry John, what's up?" asked Melinda.

"There be someone at the roadblock that wants to be let in. The Staff Sargent at the checkpoint wants to speak at ye. He's been trying for some time and finally gave up. He called me on the radio." The head of security handed her the radio in his hand.

"Just press the button on the side when you want to talk." said John kindly.

"This is Melinda Chase." Melinda said.

"Ms. Chase, this is Staff Sargent Ruiz at the main checkpoint. We have a Jessica Chase and a Greg Austin that want to be admitted."

"Yes, please, let them in!"

"I'm sorry, Ma'am, I can't do that." said the gatekeeper.

"What are you talking about. Let them in, that's an order!" said Melinda in a raised voice.

"Ma'am, the young lady is infected. I can let the Mr. Austin in, but the young lady is out of the question. I have my orders!"

"Mom! Let me in! What's going on! I just have a cold! That's all!" Melinda could hear Jessica's voice through the radio.

"Step back Miss." The Staff Sargent demanded.

"Look. This is the CDC, we have quarantine quarters, let her in and we'll put her in there until she's tested for the virus. Please Sargent Ruiz, she's my daughter!" pleaded Melinda.

"I'm sorry Ms. Chase. My orders are explicit. No one showing signs of the virus are to be admitted, period. Would you like me to let the man in?" Sargent Ruiz asked again.

"Let me speak to your commanding officer! Now!" Melinda demanded.

"I have no one else above me that I can reach Ma'am. As far as I know they're all dead."

"Will your Commander in Chief do?! How about I get him on the line and tell him that his cousin's daughter was not allowed into the CDC for treatment by a Staff Sergeant on a power trip!" Melinda bluffed, sort of. She did have a line to the President, but they were no relation. He didn't know that though.

"OK. OK. Ma'am, no need for that. I'll let them pass. But only when a containment unit meets them and escorts them to the quarantine facility." Sergeant Ruiz surrendered to her demands, but not without reasserting his position.

"Fine, I'll send one down right away. Thank you Sargent Ruiz."

"My pleasure Ma'am. Miss, Sir, please wait over there." He said to Greg and Jessica who had a seat under the awning where the rain continued to fall.

Melinda handed the radio back to John Mckenzie and said. "John, could you see to it please?"

"Absolutely Melinda, no problem!" John replied and headed out the door.

John Mckenzie and two men, all in hazmat suits escorted Greg and Jessica to the third floor wing of the CDC where medical facilities complete with wards, beds and surgical rooms awaited. Both guests were stripped, rinsed in chemical agents, rinsed with saline solution and air dried. They were provided new sterile clothes and left in separate rooms. Blood samples were taken and the doors were locked and John and the two men left.

The blood samples were taken to Noah in the secure lab where he put them in the containment tank and placed a drop of each on separate slides. Greg's was clean. Jessica's was not. She had the virus. Noah picked up the phone and called Melinda.

"Hi Melinda. It's Noah. I have the results of the blood test of your ex-husband and your daughter." Noah said in his professional voice, not giving away his emotions.

"Are they OK?" asked Melinda

"Greg is OK…."

Melinda held her breath and put her hand over her mouth in anticipation.

"… but I'm sorry to say that Jessica has the virus." Noah said sadly.

"No!" screamed Melinda. "Not my daughter!" she broke into tears. "I told her to get here. I knew the virus was coming to Atlanta with the rain. I told her to stay out of the rain! But she had to get her father! If only she hadn't delayed." Melinda sobbed into the phone as she slouched in her chair.

"Melinda" Noah began "We'll do everything we can for her."

"That's great Noah. We can watch her die, just like everyone else!"

"Melinda, I understand how you feel. But you really must get control of yourself. Your daughter will need you now, more than ever."

"I'm sorry Noah, it's not you I'm mad at. I just don't like losing! Not only have do we no way to defeat this virus that is raining terror down upon the world, but now my daughter has a death sentence on her. If we can't find a way to kill this virus, it's just a matter of time until there is no one left on the planet."

"We will Melinda! I know we are not alone. There are labs all over the world trying to find a way to fight this thing. Someone will come up with a way. I am sure of it!" Noah said trying to sound optimistic.

"I hope so Noah. Thanks for setting me straight." Melinda sighed, stood up, straightened her skirt and blouse and said, "I better go tell her."

"Don't give up Melinda, I won't!" Noah said finally and hung up.

Melinda took a deep breath checked her face in her compact mirror, combed her hair and headed out of the office.

After a short trip in the elevator and a quick thank you to John Mckenzie whom she passed in the hall, she was in front of her daughter's room. The airtight door had a window in it and an intercom below that.

"Jessica?" Melinda said as she pushed the button. Jessica was sitting on the bed, elbows on her knees a blood stained Kleenex in her hand.

"Mom?" she said shakily, "I've got it don't I." she asked, for an instance she was again the little girl Melinda remembered.

"Oh, Jessica!" Melinda started. "Yes honey, I'm afraid so."

Jessica stood and straitened her clothes, not unlike her mother did, walked over to the window and said "Well that's just great. Do you have a cure yet? The great Melinda Chase at the Center for Disease Control going to save the day?!" she said, once again the defiant youth.

"No, I haven't, but we haven't given up. Don't you either! We will find a way to beat this thing. I promise you." Melinda said ignoring the sarcasm in her daughter's voice. She realized that it was her way of coping with the fear that she felt as well.

"I'm sorry Mom. I guess I'm a little scared." Jessica said as she pressed her hand against the window.

"I know Jessica, I am too. I've got the best people I know working on it. Don't worry." Melinda said hoping to calm her daughter, and herself. She placed her hand on the window as well, their hands barely separated by the glass.

"How is Daddy?" asked Jessica.

"He's fine. No virus." Melinda couldn't hide the bitterness in her voice.

"Mom, it's not his fault! Don't you blame him for this. I did everything I could to stay out of the rain and I didn't drink any water. I don't know where I got it from."

Melinda sighed, "I know Jessica. But why couldn't you have been spared?"

"Who knows Mom? What difference does it make? If you don't find a cure, we're all dead eventually. How much bottled water is there in the world anyway? It'll run out won't it? Then what?" Jessica asked.

"Then the virus wins, and I won't let that happen!" Melinda said, then "I have to get back to work. The doctors will be by soon to make you comfortable. Be nice. OK?"

"Sure Mom. Go save the world." Jessica said sarcastically and threw herself on the bed.

Melinda took a deep breath, turned and headed back to her office. "There must be an answer somewhere!" She thought to herself. "There just has to be."

Chapter 31

As he became aware of his surroundings he realized that he was lying down in a hospital bed and that someone was in the room with him. Dr. Thomas Katz looked over to see Ruth Nixon asleep a chair beside his bed. He tried to speak but he couldn't find his voice, his mouth was dry and he had oxygen tubes in his nose. When Thomas felt that her hand was in his he gently squeezed it. She awoke instantly and leaned forward.

"Oh thank God!" she said with deep emotion, visibly relieved that he was now awake. "I was so worried!" Nurse Nixon raised a water bottle to his mouth and he drank it eagerly.

"What happened?" he croaked through dry lips.

"You were shot, remember?" he nodded. "Afterwards I took you to surgery and managed to clean you up, the bullet passed right through your chest just under the collar bone; thank goodness it didn't hit any of your vital organs."

"It's quiet, where is everybody?" asked Dr. Katz. "I remember now, there was a crowd of people stealing supplies."

"Yes. They ignored us once you were shot. The emergency room is still wide open, but there is no one there now. Everyone's gone. We are on the fourth floor, in the cancer ward. It's pretty much you and I. I think everyone else has left." Nurse Nixon walked over to the window and looked out into the night. "The city is almost dark except for the fires." As she looked out she could see a police car going by on a street miles away, its lights illuminating the buildings in blue and red flashes. "There is some activity, but there are no raging crowds. The rain has finally stopped. I can see the moon now between the clouds."

"Thank you Ruth for your help. I couldn't have made it without you." said Thomas sincerely.

"You are very welcome Dr. Katz." She said as she sat in the chair at his side again.

"Please call me Thomas. I think we're beyond formalities now, don't you?" he said as he took her hand in his again.

"Yes I suppose we are." She replied. Ruth lifted his hand to her lips and kissed it and then held it against her face. A tear fell from her eye as she smiled. Ruth had always felt that they would be together one day, but put those feelings aside because they worked so closely together.

Thomas was mildly surprised by the show of affection, but not put off. He liked Ruth and he too put his feelings aside for the sake of professionalism. Now they could relax. If the virus would eventually get them, at least they could enjoy each other's company now.

"Well, I guess we're going to be here for a while. Can I get you anything else?" asked Ruth. "I'm going to go and see if there's any more water about. That's the last one."

"I'll come with you." Thomas said, trying to sit up but a wave of dizziness hit him and he lay down again.

"I don't think so. You just lay there for a few hours and rest. You've lost a lot of blood, and it will take time to recover." Ruth ordered.

"Something to read maybe?" he asked.

"OK." Ruth walked out of the room and came back with a stack of magazines, and put them on his lap. "Will these do?" she asked with a smile.

"Sure. Thanks" he said. He began looking through the stack.

"I'll see you in a few minutes." Ruth said and left the room.

Thomas found Time magazine with a headline of "Technology – A cure for cancer?" Thomas put down the rest of the magazines and flipped to the article.

There was a man named Matthew Parker who had experimented with using micro-machines called nanobots, to reportedly cure cancer. He was going to conduct a human trial of a procedure where nanobots were injected into a subject and would rid the person of cancer. Thomas finished the article and looked at the picture of the man in his California home.

Matthew Parker appeared confident. He was tanned with an easy smile and was sitting on a piece of exercise equipment with a towel around his neck, barely covering his muscular body. Behind him Thomas could see through a floor to ceiling window the beautiful view of a California valley.

"Is it possible?" Thomas thought to himself. "Could this technology defeat the alien virus, where medicine could not?"

Thomas struggled to a sitting position on the bed. After the dizziness subsided he reached for the phone. He dialed directory assistance. After listening for the voice automated prompts he said "Center for Disease Control, Atlanta, Georgia." The phone began ringing on the other end.

"Please enter the extension of the party you are calling, or if you know the name, please say the name."

"Melinda Chase" said Thomas.

"Thank you, please wait while I dial that party"

The phone rang. It continued to ring several times before he heard Melinda say *"You have reached Melinda Chase. I am not available right now, please leave a detailed message and I'll get back to you as soon as I can. Thank you!"*

After the beep, Thomas said. "Melinda, this is Dr. Thomas Katz. I don't know if you will get this, but this is urgent. I have an idea that might kill this horrible virus. Contact Matthew Parker in California. He has created nanobots that can kill cancer cells. My thought is that they could be reprogrammed to fight this virus! If you get this message, please try to get him. Please let me know what you think. My number is 206-364-0500, my extension is 323. Thanks!"

Thomas hung up the phone and lay back down sweating and exhausted. He prayed that Melinda would get the message.

Chapter 32

"Hey! Jim! Someone's coming." said Bobby to his friend. Jim didn't respond. He was hunched over against the passenger window, apparently watching for vehicles.

They were parked in the police cruiser across the street from the gate to Matthew Parker's house. Bobby could see headlights coming up the road. The headlights illuminated the rain as it continued to fall in sheets onto the slick road and splashed in the puddles formed there.

The car could be heard shifting gears as it slowed and stopped in front of the gate. The gate started to open and Bobby started his car. He would wait until Matthew was through, and then follow him in.

Matthew waited for the gate to open enough and drove through the gate, up his driveway and beside the house to the garage. The house was dark except for the automatic flood lights that brightened the driveway and the yard as he approached the house. Maria would have gone for the day as it was close to ten o'clock at night.

He pressed a button on the remote in the car's dashboard and the garage door opened. He parked inside, got out of the Crossfire and opened the door to his house. He was about to close the garage door using the button on the wall when he was startled by a police cruiser screeching to a stop inches behind his. The driver's side door flew open and he recognized the mercenary instantly.

"Just you wait a minute!" said Bobby, pointing a very large pistol at Matthew. "We have some unfinished business."

"Whatever you say buddy." Matthew said. "But who's we?" he asked.

Bobby looked over at the other side of the car and expected Jim to be there pointing his own weapon at Matthew. He wasn't there. He dipped his head and looked into the car. Jim hadn't moved.

"Jim! Come on mate, let's go!" he said urgently. He unknowingly lowered his gun a few inches and Matthew took the opportunity to jump forward and kicked the car door into Bobby.

The gun went skittering over the top of the car and into the driveway. Matthew looked for any weapon he could find and picked up a shovel. Pointing it at Bobby he said. "Look, don't we have enough going on with the worldwide plague that we can put aside our differences? I mean come on. You're exposed by standing in the rain, your buddy obviously has the virus, give me a break!" Matthew reasoned.

"Don't try and weasel your way out of a beating mate, you won't get out of it that easy with your fancy talk. That's a good one though, ooooh, worldwide plague. Ha ha" he said sarcastically with a laugh.

"Take a look at your friend will you? Maybe we can help him?" Matthew asked.

Bobby leaned into the car, reached over and pulled his friend towards him. "Jim, you OK?" What he saw he'd never forget. Jim stared at him through vacant bulging eyes, his swollen protruding tongue dripping blood that had poured from his nose. Bobby had seen a lot of violence in his time in the British SAS, but he had never seen anything so grotesque before. His good friend of many years was dead from an enemy he couldn't fight.

Bobby straightened up and standing in the rain that would eventually kill him said. "He's dead." As he spoke he broke into a violent coughing spell. When he pulled his hand away from his mouth which he had instinctively covered, the blood in his hand mixed with the rain that was falling. He looked up at Matt. A man who was afraid of nothing in his life, said with fear in his voice for the first time. "It's too late for Jim, but maybe you can help me?"

"I'm willing to try." said Matt, putting down the shovel. "Come inside."

Matt walked into his house and Bobby followed.

Matt said "There's some workout clothes through there" he pointed to his training room, "we're close to the same size so the outfits should fit you."

"OK, thanks." Bobby said as he went to find the clothes.

"You can take a shower if you want. The damage is done already, and you might feel better afterwards." Suggested Matt.

"Alright. Nice digs mate." said Bobby as he picked up a pair of shorts and a Karate uniform from the rack and came back out of the training room. "Shower?" he asked.

"Through the bedroom, on the left." Matt answered as he sat down at his desk and opened his laptop. He checked his inventory of carbon and his supply of the radioactive isotope for tracking the nanobots. He still had a few ounces of carbon and a few grams of the isotope so he could create more nanobots if he needed to. He also had several hundred nanobots in storage from his cancer research, but they would have to be reprogrammed to identify and track the new virus.

Matt wondered what the new virus looked like. He would need a sample of rain water, or of blood to see the virus and program the nanobots. He walked into his makeshift lab off the kitchen and found a pair of rubber gloves. He put on a surgical mask, goggles and a pair of rubber gloves. He pulled a sterile tube out of a drawer and a pipette from a shelf. Once he was back out in the garage he picked up an umbrella and headed out to Bobby's car.

Jim was still in the same position that Bobby had left him in. Matt opened the passenger door and after securing the umbrella in the window, reached inside to take a blood sample from Jim's nose.

Matt went back inside and into the lab. He tossed the pipette in the trash and took the sample to his workbench where he created a slide from the blood. He put the sample under a microscope and viewed it on a computer monitor.

He could see individual blood cells and virus cells. Using a fine instrument he separated the blood cells from the virus cells and zoomed in. When he had only one virus cell in view he pressed a key on the computer keypad and snapped a photo of the virus. He gave the picture a filename of alien-virus and saved it.

Matt brought up his nanobot program and referenced the picture's filename. Then he went to the fridge and took out a tube of nanobots. He placed them in an interface coupling device that connected the computer to the tube of nanobots through a series of wires. Matt typed in a command on the computer that executed his program that would reprogram the nanobots to recognize the alien virus. He hit run and a window came up on his computer screen that showed a green progress bar that quickly went up to 10 percent and then 11 percent. Time remaining showed 2 hours 10 minutes. The tube of nanobots began to glow and pulse.

Matt checked his watch and made a mental note to check back in two hours. That would be around midnight. He went out to the training room to see Bobby drinking bottled water and looking out at the view through the window. "It's stopped raining." He said.

"That's good." said Matt. "Maybe now people can get out and get some fresh air."

"For all the good it'll do them." Bobby said discouragingly, thinking of his friend in the car. "So what do we do now?" he asked.

Matt said "We wait. It'll take about two hours for the nanobots to be programmed to recognize the alien virus. Once that's complete we can inject you with them and hopefully see instant results."

"Do I have two hours?" Bobby asked.

"I don't know, um, what's your name?" Matt asked in turn.

"Robert Spears. My friends call me Bobby. My enemies don't call me anything, they don't live long enough."

"I gathered that. How long have you worked for Gerald Pharmaceuticals Bobby?"

"I don't. I work for Albert Jennings. He works for Gerald as a kind of fixer. I am under contract to him. Actually this is my first assignment with him. I am what you call a freelance soldier." Bobby explained with a smile.

"A mercenary" Matt stated

"If you like, although I prefer freelance, it has a nice professional appeal, don't you think?"

"It really doesn't matter now what it's called. I'm sure you are paid well." said Matt.

"Well enough. However, not as well as you it appears." Bobby said as he nodded towards the pool and the well outfitted training room.

"I am not paid. All this was from a good investment and I don't have to work now. What I do is pure research for the benefit of mankind. I have no ambition to be rich or famous." Matt said.

"I see. Well Mr. Philanthropist, Let's hope your work bears fruit. For my sake, and for the sake of all humanity." Bobby said sincerely then started to cough again.

"As you say." Agreed Matthew who put his hand on Bobby's back to comfort him and looked at his watch. One hour and 55 minutes left.

Chapter 33

The leased Lear jet made a low pass of the airstrip at Winslow, Arizona. The pilot checked out the runway to make sure there were no obstructions and radioed his intentions to land to local traffic.

The jet then began a gentle climb and an easy circle around the airport to line up with runway 29.

"Here we are my dear!" said Dr Francis Magee to his wife Monique, our new home. Winslow Arizona."

Monique looked out the window. There was no movement on the ground. No cars or people that she could see.

"Are you sure it's OK here? I see nothing moving down there." Monique asked.

"Of course it's safe my dear, I had it checked out. We have a lovely ranch house outside of town with our own water supply, air conditioning and solar power. We'll be just fine!"

"OK, thank you Francis, I'm just a bit nervous."

"Not to worry amour" Francis said comforting his wife.

The jet continued its gentle curve and then leveled off in line with the runway. The airspeed slowed and the nose came up as the flaps and wheels were lowered for landing.

Suddenly the gentle descent was interrupted by a sharp lurch to the left and then to the right. Then the engines roared back to life as the jet climbed into the sky at an ever increasing rate.

"What in the world?!" exclaimed Dr. Magee as he was pushed back in his seat. He struggled to his feet and worked his way up the aisle to the cockpit door. By the time he got there the jet was almost vertical. As he hung on to the door to the cockpit he became weightless as the jet reached the apex of its climb and stalled at 12000 feet with the engines screaming their complaint. He was pushed forward as the jet began its rapid nose down descent. Francis struggled to open the cockpit door as Monique screamed hysterically.

He was finally able to open the cockpit door and was shocked by what he saw. The pilot was in his seat, strapped in, but his hands were hanging at his sides. No one was flying the jet. Dr. Magee lifted the pilots head and saw the signs of the alien virus. Bulging eyes and protruding tongue. The pilot was infected.

He instinctively got into the copilot seat and strapped himself in. He had never flown before, but had seen enough movies to know that he had to pull back on the control yolk. Through gritted teeth and pulling with all he had he cried "Come on! Come on!" but he could see the ground coming up at him spinning at an ever increasing rate.

Little did Dr. Francis Magee know that he was doing exactly the wrong thing. The Lear jet was in a spiral dive now and a trained pilot knows that the yolk should be in neutral position and opposite rudder applied to recover from it. Pulling back on the yolk had no effect. Dr. Francis Magee joined his wife in a scream of frustration.

Albert Jennings watched from the airport and smiled as the Lear jet continued its spiral dive until it made a spectacular fireball in the Arizona desert. His plan had worked. Exchanging the pilot's bottled water with a bottle of rainwater yesterday morning had done the trick. He wasn't exactly sure how fast the virus worked, but took a chance. He could always finish off the job on the ground if he had to.

His smile turned into a grin as he lit his cigar again. "I'll enjoy that ranch house. Thank you Dr. Magee!" he said and chuckled to himself as he blew clouds of smoke into the air and walked towards the terminal and out the gate to his SUV.

Chapter 34

The rain continued to fall, but the sky seemed to be turning from an angry black mass to grey and white and the drops were more of the usual size that Seattle was used to; the familiar drizzle of the Pacific North West.

The Humvee moved through the streets of Seattle, moving noisily around cars that had been abandoned. Shoving some out of the way, and going around others. The bodies however they just rode right over. They were strewn throughout the street like someone had thrown them from the back of a truck, men, women and children.

When the Humvee arrived outside Wal-Mart, it just kept driving, right through the front doors and into the entrance way. The engine was silenced and the doors opened. Three men got out in military garb and started through the aisles, one with a shopping cart the others watching for threats.

As they got to the beer and wine section they started to load up. That's when two men appeared, one with a shotgun, one with a handgun. The man with the shotgun appeared to be an employee, at least he was wearing a blue Wal-Mart vest but it appeared a little small for him.

"Hey losers this is our store! Get out!" he shouted.

The other man had on a leather jacket with a flaming skull on the back and appeared to be a biker of sorts. He held a handgun and pointed it at the soldiers. "Yeah!" he said.

The three soldiers stopped, stood up and faced the two men.

"I don't think so buddy. Take a hike before you regret ever waking up this morning." said one of the soldiers seriously.

The Wal-Mart guy raised his shotgun but he never had a chance to fire. The men cut him and his biker friend down in a short and one sided firefight.

Without saying another word the soldiers finished loading their cart and headed back to the front of the store. When they got there, their Humvee was missing. The front door was broken open from their entry but their vehicle was nowhere in sight.

They ran outside, guns at the ready and were greeted by three soldiers who used hand to hand combat techniques to disarm them and had them on the ground spread eagled in seconds.

"I suggest Boyo, that *you* take a hike!" said Connie. "Get yourselves out o' the rain. It's poison y'know!"

"OK. Take it easy!" said one. With that Connie's team let them up and they ran away.

"Bloody amateurs!" Jones said.

"Let's get moving. Pick up their guns. They'll come back with more men. You can count on it. Load up both Humvees and let's get back to base." Connie ordered.

In a few minutes the two Humvees rolled away carrying first aid, food, camping supplies and as much bottled water as they could carry. They encountered no resistance as they travelled through the streets of Seattle. It was a bit eerie. No one at Starbucks; no one driving to work; no one walking or cycling or rushing about. The city had died. Surely someone survived. It had only been a 24 hours since the virus hit Seattle.

As they rolled down the road they saw an American flag hanging out of the fourth floor window of the Midwest Medical Center Hospital. It was unusual because it was hanging out a broken window that didn't usually open. Moore spotted it and pointed to Connie.

"Do you think we should check it out?" he asked.

"Why not?" asked Connie and signaled to the trailing vehicle the command to stop.

After they dismounted, they formed a three man skirmish. Connie was in the lead, Jones in the middle and Moore behind. All sides were covered with their weapons as they progressed from the Humvees, through the broken Emergency room doors and through the waiting room to a set of stairs. The waiting room was a shambles as if someone had ransacked the place. Little did they know that that is exactly what happened.

They found a blood trail which started on a wall and went to the elevator, but decided the stairs would suffice.

Up the stairs checking all corners before cautiously proceeding, they made their way up to the fourth floor.

After they came out of the stairwell Connie called out "Hello! Is anyone there?"

"Here!" said a voice that came from down the hall. A pretty redhead peeked out of one of the rooms. "In here!" she called.

The men arrived at the doorway and entered the room. "We saw your flag out the window" said Connie.

"I knew someone would see it!" said Ruth. "I'm Ruth Nixon and this is Dr. Thomas Katz."

"Tom" said Thomas extending his had from his sitting position in the bed.

"Nice to meet you. I'm Connie, that's Moore and Jones." said Connie as he pointed to the other men who nodded as their name was said. "Are you mobile Sir?" he asked Thomas.

"I can make it." said Thomas.

"Then let's go!" Connie said and turned to leave.

"Wait a minute! What about the others!"

"Others?" asked Connie.

"I'll show you." Nurse Nixon said as she went through the door and turned right.

She went by each room in turn and greeted those inside. One or two people occupied the rooms, each one in a hospital bed, many were alert and sitting up, but a few were sleeping.   Some were hooked up to IV lines and others were not.

Many were missing hair and eyebrows. They were all cancer patients in various stages of treatment, seventeen in total.

"You've got to be kidding me." said Moore out loud.

"Miss Nixon. Are these patients mobile?" Connie asked.

"They should be. Mr. Jones probably can't move without assistance, but the rest should be able to walk short distances until they gain their strength back." Ruth replied.

"Jesus, Mary and Joseph!" exclaimed Jones. "How are we going to get these people to the house?" he asked.

"We'll take the supplies and come back for them." Connie answered.

"What about the goon squad out there?" asked Moore.

"Goon squad?" asked Thomas, who had followed them down the hall.

"Let's just say there were some unsavory characters at the Wal-Mart store and we convinced them to move along.   We sort of helped ourselves to their transportation and they will be looking for us with some buddies to even the score I suppose." Connie explained.

"Great." said Thomas sarcastically.

"Look my boy, if you'd prefer we leave you here, I can easily oblige." said Connie, getting a bit offended by Dr. Katz's tone.

"It's not that Connie. It's just that I hate violence. I've seen enough death in my life." Thomas explained.

"I see. Well, Boyo, we'll try to avoid any more nasty business if we can. In the meantime, Jones will stay with you and keep watch, while Moore and I head back to the house and drop off the supplies. We'll come back and get you all as soon as we can. It'll take about 2 hours. Will you be OK until then?" Connie asked.

"We'll be fine and we all are very grateful that you showed up. Trust me on that." said Thomas.

"Jones, stay here and keep watch. Are you copacetic?" Connie asked Jones with a pat on the shoulder.

"Sure thing Sergeant." said Jones.

"Thank you so much you guys! It's so wonderful to see you and to know that you'll help us! Where are we going exactly?" asked Ruth.

"Cougar Mountain, my friend has a nice house there where you'll be safe." Explained Connie.

"OK" she said.

"OK. We'll be back in no time!" Connie declared "Let's move out." He ordered and Moore followed him down the hall and down the stairs to the Humvees.

They each got in one, started them up and started back to the house. "Stay on 7!" ordered Connie on his hand held radio. "Got it." said Moore. "10-4" said Jones. The Humvees turned the corner.

Watching from the building across the street, three men in camouflage outfits stepped out of the shadows. A dozen more men in various attire, all with rifles or handguns, came out of a back lane between storefronts.

One of the men looked up at the American flag hanging from the fourth floor window. "Let's see what's up there!" said their leader. They each had on some form of military wear and were obviously a militia of some sort. Some wore gas masks, others welding helmets, some clear visors each with some protection from the rain.

They started across the street, their boots splashing in the puddles as they stepped over dead bodies. The leader saw the open emergency doors and lead the men inside.

Chapter 35

Melinda arrived back at her desk and asked Charlotte to call a meeting in her office. Within minutes a weary team came in.

Noah was looking haggard. Jacob looked pretty much the same as usual in his wool vest. Sam and Rhonda came in together looking like they hadn't slept in days. Charlotte arrived with her laptop and sat down at the desk. She looked like she had just come from the hair dresser, prim, proper and pressed.

"Well I hope someone has good news for us!" Melinda said trying to sound up beat.

Noah looked at his hands. Jacob cleared his throat. Sam looked at Rhonda and nodded.

Rhonda said "Melinda? I have some good news. We've uploaded the meteor trajectory that we received from Derek Manheim. It confirms your thought that the virus is indeed alien in nature. We've mapped out the spread on a graphic..." she nodded at Sam who pulled up the hologram. "...as you can see the meteor's eight pieces coincide directly with the viruses spread around the world, following the northern and median jet streams."

"There seems to be some holes in the map. Are those areas virus free?" asked Noah.

"Yes, for now." Answered Sam for Rhonda but she continued "The areas in the lower most parts of the southern hemisphere are not yet affected by all reports. Argentina, South Africa, and southern Australia are all uncontaminated. Some parts of the Middle East have not yet had rainfall, so they are free as well. North Eastern Arizona has also been spared."

"Well that is some good news for the most part." said Melinda, then asked. "Anyone else?"

Charlotte cleared her throat. "Excuse me Melinda, I know you weren't exactly asking me, but…"

"No, go ahead Charlotte, if it's good news let's hear it" said Melinda.

"I knew that you have all been so busy and I felt like I wasn't doing much to help, so I hope you don't mind, but I went through your voice mails Melinda." Charlotte said sheepishly.

"Go on." Melinda encouraged her to keep going.

"Well, there is one from Dr. Katz in Seattle, Washington. He has an idea, well, it sounds farfetched, but, um, well, I guess you should all just hear it and see what you think." Charlotte finished.

The speaker in the ceiling began to play the message and Dr. Katz's voice could be clearly heard…

"Melinda, this is Dr. Thomas Katz. I don't know if you will get this, but this is urgent. I have an idea that might kill this horrible virus. Contact Matthew Parker in California. He has created nanobots that can kill cancer cells. My thought is that they could be reprogrammed to fight this virus! If you get this message, please try to get

him. Please let me know what you think. My number is 206-364-0500, my extension is 323. Thanks!"

"Thank you Charlotte. What do you all think?" asked Melinda.

Jacob said "Sounds a bit like something from Star Trek don't you think?"

"I'll try anything to beat this thing. Lord knows I've tried everything else I can think of" said Noah.

Sam said. "Sound cool. If there is any possibility of it working I say let's try it."

"Me too!" said Rhonda.

"OK. Charlotte, have you tried to find Matthew Parker in California?" asked Melinda.

"Yes, there are 19 hits on Google and only one that sounds reasonable. He lists his occupation as research scientist. I checked the white pages for his name and he's listed in Los Gatos, California but the number is unlisted." Charlotte answered.

"He could be dead by now you know." said Jacob, stating the obvious.

"Jacob, let's not think that way just yet. I'll call my brother in Connecticut; maybe he has a way to get his number." Melinda said.

"I'll try to hack into the AT&T database and see if I can find it that way too." said Sam enthusiastically.

"Well, whatever it takes folks. Let me know as soon as you get his number and we'll meet again. Thanks everyone." Melinda dismissed the meeting and everyone went out talking to each other with various levels of enthusiasm.

"Charlotte?" said Melinda catching Charlotte's eye.

"Mel?" she asked.

"Could you try to reach Dr. Thomas Katz in Seattle and thank him?" Melinda asked.

"I'm sorry Mel, I've tried several times and there has been no answer. I cannot get the police either. I fear the worst, I'm afraid." Charlotte said sadly.

"Oh dear, that's too bad." Melinda said sincerely. "He probably saved us all. Thanks Char." She concluded.

"You're welcome. I'm so sorry." She said again.

"We're all at risk Charlotte. It's not your fault."

"Thanks Mel." She said and left the room.

Melinda picked up the phone and called her brother Frank. The phone rang several times and Frank finally answered.

"Hello?" Frank said.

"Hi Frank it's Melinda. Did everyone get there safe? Are you all OK?" asked Melinda.

"Yes, we're fine here. We're secure and have enough food for and water for two or three weeks if we ration it. Terry and Bill didn't come in and we can't get them on the phone. Nobody else from the second shift came in. We fear the worst. There were people being robbed in at a roadblock we breached. They were stealing water and food from each other. It's a real mess here. We're safe though. I've barricaded us in and we're in the Network Operations Center which is about as secure as we can get. As long as we have power, we're OK. If the power goes out, we'll have to climb to the higher levels because we'd suffocate in the NOC. So far we have air conditioning and lights so we're good. What's happening out there?" He asked. "Are you guys making headway against this virus thing?"

"I'm glad to hear that you are safe. Actually, that's why I'm calling. I need to get in touch with Matthew Parker in Los Gatos California. He may have some technology we could use against this virus. I was hoping that you could find his number for us?"

"What am I directory assistance? Let me check, hang on." said Frank and put her on hold where she heard slightly distorted music from the 60's blaring in her ear.

"Frank?" she called out, but it was too late. She'd have to endure 'You've Really Got Me' by the Kinks for a few minutes until Frank returned.

Frank sat at his console and opened a new black and white window on the view screen. Inside he typed a few command codes and a listing of Matthew Parkers in California began to scroll up the screen. He highlighted the one in Los Gatos, and it zoomed in to more detail. He picked up the phone again and said "Matthew Parker, on Alma Ridge Road, Los Gatos, California?" he asked.

"Sounds right" said Melinda.

"408-354-4807"

"Just a second, Frank, can you repeat that?" Melinda now had a pencil and paper at the ready.

"408-354-4807" Frank repeated.

"408-354-4807, got it. Thanks Frank!"

"Anything else you need?" asked Frank.

"No, thanks Frank and let me know if you need anything else too, OK?" Melinda instructed.

"Sure thing, bye Melinda."

"Bye Frank, and take care."

"You too." said Frank.

Melinda hung up the phone and dialed the number for Matthew Parker. The phone rang and was answered pretty quickly. "Matt Parker." Matt said.

"Matthew Parker, the scientist who cured cancer?" Melinda asked

"Look, I don't know how you got this number, but I'm in no mood for prank calls!" Matt said irritably.

"I'm sorry Mr. Parker, I didn't mean to come across as a prank call. This is Melinda Chase of the Center for Disease Control. I was hoping that you could help us."

"Help you how?" asked Matt guessing the answer.

"With this virus that is killing millions of people around the world. You've heard of it by now I hope?"

"Yes of course."

"I was wondering if your procedure that works for cancer, could be adopted for use against this virus?" Melinda asked.

"I'll let you know in about 20 minutes." said Matt without humor.

"What?" said Melinda incredulously.

"I've already injected my nanobots into a test subject. If it works he'll be free of the virus in 20 minutes."

"Are you serious?" asked Melinda again.

"Very." said Matt exhausted.

"That's amazing Mr. Parker! If it works, can it be replicated?"

"Yes, but let's see if it works first. OK?" suggested Matt.

"Certainly. Will you call me on my cell phone when you know for sure?" asked Melinda and gave him the number.

"I'd be happy to Melinda. Let's all pray that it does work." Matt said.

"I'm with you Mr. Parker."

"Matt."

"Matt. Thanks, I'll wait for your call." said Melinda.

"I'll let you know in twenty, goodbye."

"Bye"

Melinda hung up the phone and asked everyone to come back into her office as they waited for her cell phone to ring.

Chapter 36

Matthew hung up the phone and went back to the lab where he found Bobby reclining in a comfortable chair.

"How are you doing?" he asked Bobby.

"I'm fine mate. It burns a bit where you injected me, but I've had much worse." Bobby replied.

Matt put on a mask and surgical gloves and put on a pair of safety glasses. He walked over to Bobby and looked at his eyes. They were already showing signs of infection. The blood vessels were red and his eyes appeared under pressure as if they were being pushed out from behind.

"If this works you should be feeling relief pretty soon. Do you want some pain medication?" asked Matt as he stepped back.

"No sir, I can handle it." Bobby winced a bit as he felt a burning sensation in his throat. It had started in his chest and warmth mixed with pain seemed to be spreading throughout his torso, up his neck and into his head. His head felt as if it would explode as the nanobots reached his sinuses and he groaned and grimaced as they worked behind his eyes.

"I – can – see – them!" he said through his teeth as the nanobots entered his eyes. He could see them as they moved in front of his vision like spiders floating in a pool of water.

"This – is – fun." Bobby said sarcastically as the pain and burning continued. Then as fast as it started it stopped and Bobby said "Oh! It stopped."

Matt took another look at Bobbys eyes. They were still red, but the swelling had subsided. "How do you feel?" Matt asked.

"I feel good." Bobby answered and stood up from the chair. "I feel great in fact." He said.

"Alright, let's take a blood sample." Matt suggested.

"Cool" said Bobby as he sat down again and gave Matthew his arm.

Matthew pulled a syringe out of a drawer, removed the sterile wrapper and found a vein in the muscular arm of Bobby. He only pulled a couple of milliliters of blood and set a drop on a slide. Under the microscope and visible on the computer's monitor, were several healthy blood cells, several damaged blood cells, two or three nanobots and a few pieces of the virus. Not one whole virus was shown in the drop of blood.

"Take a look Bobby." Matt said. "The virus has been destroyed. You can see the pieces floating by there…" he pointed "and there" he pointed again. "These are healthy blood cells and these are ones that have already been destroyed. I'd say it worked like a charm."

"That's marvelous! I must say I feel much better. Thank you so much." He paused, "It's too bad that Jim died when he did. He could have been saved." Bobby looked away.

"I'm sorry Bobby I guess you guys were close." Matt said.

"Somalia, Angola, Columbia, and the Falklands. We survived them all together. To be beaten by something you can't see is just so frustrating! I'm glad you've found a way to beat it." He sighed, squared his shoulders and asked "So now what?"

"Now we get the cure to the CDC and hopefully they still have the resources to disseminate the cure around the world." Matt answered.

"Alright mate, let's get to it!" said Bobby enthusiastically.

Chapter 37

"Melinda Chase" Melinda said as she answered her cell phone on speaker.

"Hi Melinda, this is Matthew Parker. It worked!" said Matt in California.

"That's wonderful! Who did you try it on?" asked Melinda.

"A new friend, Bobby Spears. I administered the nanobots that I had reprogrammed into his bloodstream and within twenty minutes he was virus free and feeling good." Matt explained.

"That's great news. How can we do the same thing. My daughter is here at the CDC and infected?" Melinda asked.

"Well, if you have a MRI, an X-ray machine, a photocopier and a computer data center with lots of storage, you can probably create the nanobots and program them to destroy the virus. I can send you the schematics, and a copy of my program. Once you have that you should be able to build the nanobot replicator device by scavenging parts from those items." Matt explained.

"How long will it take to build it?" asked Melinda.

"If you have competent engineers, probably around 18 hours." Matt answered.

"18 hours? My daughter doesn't have 18 hours." Melinda paused. "I'm sorry, I shouldn't be so selfish, it's just that I had hoped there was a way to save her in time."

"I'm sorry too. We have to figure out a way to get the information to anyone left in the world so that they can begin treating people. There should be a way to get the information out. I certainly don't have the means to do it."

"What about your brother Frank?" suggested Jacob.

"That could work I'll contact him right away, in the meantime Matt, can you send us the schematics and the program?" asked Melinda.

"Well, I can send you the schematics, but the program is too large for email. We'll need a high bandwidth data link to get the program to you."

"I'm sure that my brother Frank can help with that. Send us the schematics and we'll get started on building the device." Melinda said.

"Sure, give me your email address and I'll send it right now." Matt said.

Melinda gave Matt her email address and the call ended.

"Charlotte, can you forward the schematics to our engineering team, and to each of us?" asked Melinda.

"Will do Melinda." Charlotte said.

"We need to start working on this right away. I hope we can get this done sooner than 18 hours, for Jessica's sake." said Melinda.

Chapter 38

Frank Chase slept with his family in one of the workrooms off the NOC. They had sleeping bags and pillows that they had brought from home and some were on couches and some were on the carpeted floor. Joan's family was in the next room and all were fast asleep, finally.

When the phone rang Frank was startled and for a minute wasn't sure where he was. When he realized what was happening he stumbled to the phone at the NOC central console. "Hello?"

"Hi Frank, sorry to disturb you this early." Melinda said.

"Not to worry Mel. What's up?" said Frank sleepily.

"I think we have a cure for the virus!" Melinda said happily.

"Really? That's fantastic Melinda! That is worth being woken up for!" Frank said now fully awake. "What is it?" asked Frank.

"It's a cure for cancer developed by Matthew Parker a research scientist in California, but it can be modified to kill the virus." Melinda briefly explained.

"Amazing!" exclaimed Frank.

"Actually Frank, I need your communication skills. I want to get everyone on the phone at once and be able to transmit data as well. Can you handle that?" asked Melinda.

"Sure, who is everyone?" Frank asked.

"We need a high bandwidth link between Matthew Parker in California and our team here in Atlanta. Then we want to send a message to everyone left in the world to tell them about the cure and how to reproduce the device that creates the cure." Melinda said.

"OK, but I'll need to know who specifically to send the messages to. We can't just randomly broadcast messages to no one in particular."

"I never thought of that." Melinda paused thinking to herself.

She had a line to the President of the United States and surely he had connections with every major government. It would help to send out the message as well to medical facilities, the military and even emergency response and health organizations. Who had that information? She'd ask the team for ideas on that one.

"I'll get back to you on that Frank. For now, can you set up a data link between us and Matthew Parker?" she asked.

"I'll need his IP address, do you have it?" Frank asked in return.

"Uh, no, Hang on." Melinda said.

Melinda put Frank on hold and phoned Matt. When the call had connected, she made it a three way call.

"Frank?"

"Yes"

"Matthew?"

"Yes."

"Frank Chase this is Matthew Parker. He is the one I was telling you about. Matt, Frank has something he needs to set up a high bandwidth data connection." Melinda introduced the men to each other and indicated why they were meeting.

"Hey Matthew. What I need is the IP address and the encryption key of your router so I can establish a secure VPN between our networks. Then I can do the same thing to the Atlanta CDC. Once that is completed we can connect real-time using the same Domain. Sound good?" explained Frank after he acknowledged Matt.

"Sure." said Matthew. "Give me a second."

"Melinda, I'll need the same thing from you." said Frank.

"Sam did you get that?" Melinda said.

"Yup, working on it." said Sam.

Once all the technical details were worked out the connection was tested and secured.

"I'll need somewhere to put 4 terabytes of data." Matt said.

"I'll text you the server name via chat." said Sam.

"Cool. Got it." said Matt, then "I've begun the transfer."

"How long will it take?" asked Melinda.

"About 30 minutes at this rate" said Frank, "Hang on." Franks fingers flew on the keyboard and he stole bandwidth from other communication channels that were in the green. "Make that 10 minutes" he said proudly.

"Have you figured out what to say and where to send the announcement of the cure, the program and the instructions yet?" asked Frank.

"Not yet Frank, but getting it here and building the device will further validate Matthew's work. We're all hopeful that we can duplicate his work in less than 18 hours." Melinda said thinking of her daughter.

"There's something nagging me at the back of my mind. There was something used recently that broadcast to many different countries. Does anyone remember what it was?" said Noah.

They all scratched their heads and finally Rhonda came up with the answer. "I've got it!" she yelled, louder than she intended in her excitement she stood up. "ESONET!"

"ESONET? That was it! Dr. Frederick Schoefield used it to warn us about the meteor on a collision course with Earth. Good idea. Do you think Derek Manheim could use it to send out the message?" asked Jacob.

"I don't see why not Jacob. Good call Rhonda!" Melinda praised Rhonda in front of everyone causing Rhonda to blush and sit down again grabbing Sam's arm. She did however have a big smile on her face.

"Frank, could you get the Paranal Observatory on this call?" Melinda asked and repeated Dr. Schoefield's number, hoping Derek would answer again.

They all heard the phone ringing and the call was picked up at the other end.

"Paranal Observatory, KAMY speaking, how can we help you?" a computerized voice asked.

"KAMY! You answered the phone, that's amazing." Melinda said.

"I assure you Melinda Chase that it is very simple to do so." KAMY said. Could computers sound condescending? Melinda asked herself.

"Is Derek OK?" Melinda asked thinking the worst. "Why didn't he answer the phone?"

"He's sleeping and I didn't want to disturb him. Shall I wake him?" KAMY asked.

"Well, not necessarily, I suppose you could let him sleep. We have a cure for the virus that killed Dr.

Schoefield and the others. It has become a worldwide pandemic. We hoped that Derek could notify the world of the cure using the ESONET, and maybe even distribute instructions on how to build the device necessary to create the cure." Melinda shared with the computer.

"Well, typically that requires the Director's approval." said KAMY.

"Surely you know Dr. Schoefield is dead." said Melinda.

"Yes, so I've been told. I suppose Derek's approval would suffice under these circumstances. The ESONET has several threat levels and several levels of hierarchy of who to contact and when. Who did you have in mind to send the information to?." asked KAMY.

"I don't mean to interrupt here," said Matthew, "but we should send it to everyone in the database. We don't know at this point who is left! We might not reach anybody. I would also suggest we broadcast over the internet, over the emergency broadcast system, over ham radio, over television and radio. Everyone from a family huddled in their home, to the President in his bunker should know how to make this cure work." Matthew said with passion.

"You are absolutely right, Matthew. KAMY, we'll need it sent to everyone in your database is that possible?" asked Melinda.

"Of course." Answered KAMY.

KAMY woke up Derek, who was pleased to speak with anyone at all. He of course gave his permission to send out the message.

Frank got connected to KAMY and started transmission of the program, the data and the schematic to her server.

Melinda worked on the message that would be broadcast to the world both the written, audio and video.

Noah took care of Jessica. She was getting worse and worse every minute. He put her in a drug induced coma to alleviate the coughing and the stress on her body. He had her on a breathing machine and had her hooked up to a heart/lung machine that cleaned replaced her entire blood supply every 6 hours. This was her only hope of surviving long enough for the first test of the CDC created nanobots. Several people who worked at the CDC had already donated blood to keep her alive. Her father sat by her bedside ever since she was diagnosed and placed in a coma. According to Noah she probably could survive this way for another several hours but he gave no guarantees.

"Hey guys, I don't mean to be selfish, but is there any chance someone could pick me up? I'm good for several days here, but it's kind of freaky knowing I could be exposed by a random mosquito bite." asked Derek.

"Derek, I haven't forgotten my promise. I will mention it to the President when I speak with him again." said Melinda.

"OK, thanks Melinda." Then to KAMY, "Are you ready to send the information to the world KAMY?"

"Whenever you are all ready Derek. I will have to override the command control security, but that's no problem. I suppose you are the Director now."

"I guess so. Poor Frederick." Derek said.

"It appears that the transfer to the CDC is completed. Can you confirm Sam?" said Matth.

"Yup, it's done." replied Sam.

"OK. When it's ready to run let me know and I'll walk you guys through the connections and how to run the program." Matt said.

"Will do" Sam confirmed.

Melinda said. "OK. I guess that's it for now. Thanks everyone. I'll work on the message and speak with the President. Then I'll conference you all in again for the final transmission. I appreciate everyone's help on this. Let's all pray that this goes well."

"Amen." said Frank.

"Indeed." said Matthew.

"Amen to that!" said Derek and the rest murmured their approval.

"I'll monitor the phone here and will be ready to transmit over the ESONET when you are ready." said KAMY.

Frank told the others in the NOC the news and they celebrated together with bottled water. Frank asked

Melinda, "Hey Mel? Any chance of some of the Parker Cure finding us here?"

"The Parker Cure? I like that! You can count on it Frank!" said Melinda, "As soon as we're done testing it on Jessica, we'll send some your way."

"Thanks Mel."

"Look after all those kids Frank!" said Mel.

"Only seven, Mel, only seven." Frank said.

"Seven?"

"Oh, didn't I tell you, Maureen is expecting again!" said Frank joyously.

"That's fantastic Frank. The world will need many, many more births now." Melinda said sincerely.

"We're doing our part!" said Frank and they laughed together for the first time in days.

Chapter 39

Corporal Sean Jones moved away from the window. He had been watching the Humvees leave when he noticed movement across the street.

About a dozen men were moving towards the hospital. He didn't know their intent for sure, but he recognized three of them, so he could guess. They were the soldier wannabes from the Wal-Mart store.

The group of men moved together until they got to the emergency entrance and hesitated. Their leader, he assumed, moved forward and the group followed until they were out of sight.

Jones said to Dr. Katz and Nurse Nixon, "Looks like we're going to have some unwelcome company. I suggest you all gather in the lounge down the hall. I'll be best able to protect you there." He handed Thomas a handgun. "Just in case, Sir."

Thomas took the gun hesitantly. As a native of Israel he had served and protected his small nation during mandatory service, but always as a Doctor. He knew how to use both handguns and automatic weapons, but had never killed anyone.

"Thanks. I hope it won't be necessary." said Thomas.

"For sure'n you bet ya!" said Jones with a smile and left the room. "Quickly!" he said over his shoulder.

Jones ran to the opposite stairwell to the one that they came up. He placed a claymore in the stairwell one floor down, and one inside the doorway on this floor. He placed a trip wire across the hall with a flash-bang rigged to it about ten paces from the door.

Next he ran to the elevators called both of them to his floor and put a chair in the doors, effectively making them unavailable from any other floor.

Finally he placed a flash-bang twenty feet in front of the first stair well they had come up assuming that the enemy would use the same one and positioned himself behind the nursing station in the middle of the floor. From there he could see both ends of the hallway. He took aim at the first stairwell.

Dr. Katz and Nurse Nixon meanwhile had moved everyone to the lounge/waiting area on the floor. It was across the hall from the nursing station. It had bathrooms and enough chairs for everyone. All of them were dressed in street clothes except for Mr. Jones who was in a gown and wheelchair, IV attached.

Thomas locked both doors to the lounge from a key at the nurses' station, but the window was simple glass and could be easily shattered. The locked doors would be a small deterrent at best, but it was better than nothing. Thomas sat down with the others and pocketed the weapon. He'd use it only if necessary.

The militia moved as one, all bunched up behind their leader in the stairwell. When they got to the fourth floor he opened the door an inch or two to peek into the hallway.

Jones heard the door opening and said. "Good day sir! I'd advise caution! This floor is under our protection and you'd be well advised to leave well enough alone. Move on son. Live to fight another day!"

The man in charge of the militia, Clyde Wilson, called himself a city engineer. He was in reality in street maintenance; he was one of the guys driving the street sweepers at two in the morning down the streets of downtown Seattle.

On weekends he and his friends drank beer and did some target shooting out in the woods. Usually hilariously drunk and using automatic weapons, it was amazing no one was killed.

Clyde was the de facto leader. He was just loud enough and mean enough so that the others were a little scared of him. He seemed a bit crazy at the best of times, and having one eye looking slightly to the left didn't help to change that impression.

Now he was on a bit of a power trip. Ever since he was embarrassed in front of his men at the Wal-Mart store, he had been livid. He wasn't about to let it go.

Clyde closed the door again sweating now and wiping his forehead with his sleeve. He took a drink from his silver flask of whiskey and wiped his mouth with the back of his hand.

"Alright men. Get ready!" he commanded.

"Let's go!" he yelled and pulled the door toward him to open it. Unfortunately, the men in anticipation of the charge, had bunched up behind him and he couldn't fully open the door. Only Clyde was visible in the doorway and he couldn't raise his rifle as it was jammed behind the door. From this awkward position, Clyde struggled helplessly as he looked for his enemy expecting a bullet.

Jones, seeing the helpless expression and non-threatening position Clyde was in, set his MP5 on single fire and fired one round into the door jamb above Clyde's head. It had the desired effect and Clyde closed the door.

Firing a string of curses at his men Clyde yelled "Get back! How am I supposed to open the door you morons!"

The men sheepishly mumbled to themselves and took a few paces back. When all was ready Clyde gave the command again. "Are we ready?" he asked. Getting nods he said again "Charge!"

Clyde opened the door fully and raised his gun. Firing randomly, Clyde screamed his best war scream and charged into the hall. "Yaaaaaaah!" he yelled.

The militia followed suit, but only two could come through the door at a time and one stayed back to hold the door.

When Jones saw that this time the threat was real, he didn't hesitate. He fired three times in two seconds and the three leading men were dead on their feet with red holes in their foreheads. As they crumpled to the ground, two men behind them tumbled over their bodies and scattered for cover.

Two more went down in the doorway as Jones lethal fire found its mark. The door slammed shut as four more men sought cover in the stairwell.

Two men, one in each room on either side of the hallway looked at each other and motioned their intent with hand signals. On 'three' they came out from hiding and charged the nurses' station. One of them caught the trip wire and the flash-bang went off disorienting them.

Jones dropped them easily. It was quiet for a minute and Jones wondered if they had given up. That's when he heard a muffled explosion from the other stairwell and the screams of the men that had triggered it.

Knowing that there was another claymore set in that stairwell he moved cautiously towards the first stairwell and checked the rooms as he went. He stepped over the body of Clyde Wilson whose slightly askew and lifeless eyes wouldn't see this world again.

The stairwell proved empty but Jones set up another flash-bang just in case and walked to the outside window where the flag hung down, overlooking the street. Outside the emergency entrance below he could see the four remaining militia as they limped and staggered away, each one helping the other until they disappeared around a corner.

Jones relaxed and walked back to the lounge where he found the others in good shape. He gave the all clear through the window and when the door opened he said. "Looks safe for now. We'll just wait for Connie to get back. You may as well stay in here until we're ready. Everyone OK?"

"Yes, thank you Jones." said Thomas.

"You can call me Sean sir." said Jones.

"Sean. Then you can call me Tom." responded Thomas.

"Good." said Jones. "I've got a bit of cleanup to do, so off I go."

Jones began the unpleasant task of moving the bodies out of the hall and into one of the rooms.

Nurse Nixon looked out the window to the city of Seattle. The rain was letting up now and she could see some blue sky between the clouds. As she watched, a beam of sunshine broke through and lit up a small treed courtyard across the street where a fountain continued to flow. "Do you think we'll survive?" she asked as she heard someone enter the room.

"Of course we will. Man is resourceful. God is merciful." said Thomas and laid his hand on her shoulder and watched with her the fountain that glistened and sparkled in the brilliant beam of sunlight.

Chapter 40

"Good afternoon. I am Melinda Chase of the Center for Disease Control. Our country and our world have been devastated by a deadly virus. Millions have died and we have lost contact with major cities around the world. The President of the United States has authorized me to release information that will assist you in fighting against and killing this virus.

Matthew Parker, a research scientist in California has developed technology which creates micro machines that identify and kill the virus in the blood stream. This technology requires key components readily available in most hospitals, and it requires a program and database that is hosted on a CDC server. It also requires the components assembled and interfaced with the program.

We are making available on the CDC website the schematics for the equipment, the program and necessary data. All can be found at www.CDC.gov/virusprogram.

This message is being broadcast by Television, Radio, shortwave, internet, and ESONET.

Please work together in your community to build the equipment and execute the program to create the nanobots. Instructions on how to administer the cure is also on the website.

Humanity will survive! If you need more information or assistance please call the CDC at1-800-CDC-INFO.

Goodbye."

"How was that?" asked Melinda.

"That was very good." said Jacob.

"Awesome." said Sam.

"When can we send it out?" asked Noah.

"Right now." said Sam, "Everything is ready."

"Audio and video and text?" Melinda asked and when Sam nodded she said "OK. Let's do it! Sam can you get Frank on the line and conference in Derek and Matthew?"

"Sure thing!" said Sam.

Sam played with his PDA and the speaker phone on the desktop came to life and dialed the preloaded numbers. When all parties were on the line the call began.

"Hi everyone! Sam is sending you the message I just recorded. If possible, could we now send it out via ESONET, the Internet, Radio, Television and shortwave?"

"I can get it to the TV and Radio Stations Melinda, but there is no guarantee that anyone will be there to receive it. I sure hope so though, and if there is, I hope they relay it to other stations as well." said Frank.

Sam said. "I can take care of publishing it on the Internet on our website, in fact it's already done. I posted streaming video, audio, a transcript, and the schematic on the website. I also provided remote access to a secure server for access to the data and program. The instructions on administering the nanobots are also on the website and the server for reference."

"Good job Sam!" said Melinda.

"KAMY is ready to send out the message to ESONET." said Derek.

"Go ahead KAMY." said Melinda

"Sending it now." said KAMY.

"Sending it to TV and Radio Stations in the USA." said Frank.

"What about shortwave?" said Noah.

"Oh, I forgot about that. Ideas anyone?" asked Melinda.

"John McKenzie, he could use the military to send it out." Jacob said.

"OK. Charlotte, could you ask him to come see me?" asked Melinda.

"Sure thing Melinda." replied Charlotte and typed on her keyboard.

"How is the construction the device coming Melinda?" asked Matt.

"The engineers tell me they will have it together in a couple of hours now. They are cannibalizing other computer systems to build the interface to the nanobot tube and it's taking longer than they thought." Melinda answered.

"How is your daughter?" he asked.

"She's resting thanks to Noah. The virus is doing its best to kill her, but because she is being transfused, its progress is slow. We're hopeful that we can test your machine on her as soon as the engineers are done." said Melinda.

"That's great Melinda, I'm glad to hear that. I'm sure they'll come through. I had another thought though. The Nanobots are self-replicating. So if we had a way to distribute them with antivirus and self-replicating instructions, they could become as prolific as the virus in time, providing they had enough natural resources. The only downside is that they all wouldn't be marked for tracking and we would lose them. They could be water borne as well if we sprayed them from the air. Actually, they might just rid the water supply of viruses too! Eventually they would enter the bloodstream through the digestive tract, and provide immunity to the host." said Matt.

"Wait a minute! Couldn't they overwhelm a 'host' as you put it? Can a person get too many nanobots?" asked Jacob.

"Sure, but we can include a maximum amount per host in the program. That's a good question though Jacob." replied Matt.

"How would we distribute them in sufficient quantities to have an impact?" asked Rhonda.

"It only takes a few, say one hundred per person to fight off the virus. That's what I used on Bobby. He recovered just fine. The key is to introduce enough into the air to get about a thousand per square mile and they will seek out raw materials to replicate." explained Matt.

"What do they need"? asked Rhonda.

"They need carbon. Carbon can be found in pencils, toner, inks, graphite, charcoal, some plastics and even rubber. When a single nanobot finds a source of carbon it will replicate."

"Isn't there a chance they won't stop replicating and consume everything made of carbon? That wouldn't be good, would it?" asked Derek.

"Um, no, that would be a bad thing. We'd have to come up with a solution on that one." said Matt.

"Program the nanobots to stop replicating in 48 hours." Suggested KAMY.

"Brilliant!" said Sam.

"Yes, that will work." said Matt.

"Elementary." said KAMY.

"Could a computer be prideful?" thought Matt.

"I'll modify the program and send an update to you Sam." Matt said.

"Cool." said Sam.

"Excuse me Melinda, John McKenzie is here." said Charlotte.

John McKenzie walked in and stood at attention. "Yes Ma'am, how kin I be o' service." He asked in his Scots brogue.

Rhonda giggled a little into Sam's shoulder. She half expected him to salute!

"Can you get a message out by shortwave?" asked Melinda.

"To who Ma'am?" asked John sincerely.

"To everyone we can. I suppose we'll need to ask them to relay it as far as they can, hopefully around the world." She answered.

"I'm sorry to ask this, I've been wee bit overwhelmed on the perimeter. What's the message for?" asked John.

"No, I'm sorry John. It's to announce to the world that we have found a cure for the virus and how to administer it." Melinda explained.

"Oh, that's brilliant Ma'am. I dinna know that!" said John excited.

"Here's the message, John." said Charlotte as she gave him a printed copy of Melinda's message.

"Thank you my dear!" he said with a wink just for Charlotte.

Charlotte smiled and fixed her hair looking somewhat embarrassed. "You're welcome, John." She said.

"I'll get this to Sergeant Ruiz." John said and did an about face and left the room smartly.

"KAMY just confirmed that the message has been sent to everyone in the ESO database." said Derek.

"The Radio and TV messages are sent." said Frank.

"Fantastic job everyone. Now we wait and see what response we get."

Noah stuck his head in the door. "Melinda?" he asked.

Melinda hadn't noticed him leave. "Noah, what is it?"

"We're ready to create and program the nanobots." he answered.

Melinda stood up to leave. The others followed suit. "I guess that's it for now everyone. Thanks again for your excellent work. Maybe you should all get some rest now. I'm going with Noah to see the device work."

They all agreed that they'd like to see it work too. Matt said he'd be available to help if needed and hung up. Derek and KAMY and Frank hung up to after saying their farewells.

The call was disconnected and they all followed Noah to the second floor lab wear the engineers had constructed the device from the schematics Matthew had provided.

Chapter 41

"Is there a chance he can't hear us?" asked Lt. Col. John Reed as he drove his Wagoneer over the East Channel Bridge. They crossed the bridge and marveled at the beauty of the country side, now in full sunshine, and not a cloud in the sky.

"I think we'd be in range b'now sir." said Connie. "It could be a low battery y'know."

"Well, we'll see soon enough. Keep trying." commanded John.

"Yes Sir." said Connie, then to the handheld radio, "Jones this is Connie, come in please." When he released the button there was a burst of static, then silence. "Jones, come in Boyo!" he said again.

"out – time – ot – er - ing" came the broken reply interspersed with static.

"Say again Jones!" Connie yelled into the radio.

"It's about time you got here, I'm starving!" said Jones clearly.

"It's about time you answered me Boyo! What's wrong with your radio?" asked Connie.

"It must be low on juice. I probably should have turned it off, but I didn't think you'd be so long." Jones replied.

"I figured. OK, be there in ten.   Prepare for visitors." said Connie.

"What?" asked Jones.

"Just watch out your window son. See you soon. Over and out." said Connie.

Jones and the others watched out the window until they saw John and Connie come around the corner in the Wagoneer. They were followed by a convoy of vehicles stretching around the block.

Connie's men were on top of some of the vehicles riding shotgun. He recognized his mates cars and John's vehicles but there were school buses, city buses, dump trucks, mini-vans, cars and trucks of all shapes and sizes following behind.

"What in the world?" asked Thomas.

"Who are they all?" asked Ruth.

"I dunno." said Jones.

The vehicles pulled to a stop at the emergency entrance and people got out. Men, women and children of all sizes shapes and colors moved towards the entrance, led by John Reed.

Some started unloading supplies and bringing them inside. Connie's men coordinated the effort while John came up the stairs.

He was met by Jones who was disabling the flash-bang and trip wire.

"Expecting trouble?" he asked.

"We had a bit of trouble earlier, but nothing we couldn't handle." Jones opened the room stacked with bodies of Clyde's militia and nodded inside.

John took a look and said "Well done. Can we expect any more?"

"We should keep watch, but it won't be from this lot. I'm afraid I let four get away though." said Jones.

"That's OK. Now, we have some work to do!" said John.

"Pardon me for asking Sir, but where are all the people from? I thought we were going back to your house." asked Jones.

"We picked them up along the way. We should expect more. I have broadcast this location over shortwave to all of Washington State. I'll explain more in a minute. Where is Dr. Katz?"

"Over here." said Jones as he led John to the lounge.

"Hi! Glad you guys are OK." said John.

"Hey! Good to see you! Are we leaving now?" asked Thomas.

"Not exactly, please let me explain. This Hospital will become the command center for the distribution of the cure for the virus. We received a transmission by shortwave, relayed from the CDC in Atlanta. We now have the knowledge and should have the means to build the equipment we need right here in this hospital."

"Do you mean the nanobots?" asked Thomas?

"Yes. You know about them?" said John incredulously.

"Yes. Well, sort of. It was my idea. No, that's not quite right. It was Matthew Parker's idea to build the nanobots, but I suggested that it could be used to fight the virus. I left a message for Melinda Chase at the CDC." Thomas explained.

"That's who sent out the message!" John said. "Well, whoever gets the credit, we have work to do. We have the plans for the device and we have to build it, create the nanobots and start treating people. We can have immunity, once the nanobots are in our system."

"That means that we can drink the water then?" said Ruth. "Once we're vaccinated, I mean?"

"Yes, that makes sense." said Thomas, "Well what can I do to help?"

"We'll need to cannibalize parts from these items here." John gave Thomas the plans, and then said, "You can be in charge of getting them because of your familiarization with the Hospital."

"I'll get people organized. Ruth, have you searched the whole hospital for survivors?" asked John.

"No, only the first five floors; most of them had been cleared out either voluntarily, or by looters." Ruth answered.

"OK. We'll do a full search. I'll get someone on that too." John said, and turned away calling to Connie to get to work. He slapped Connie on his back and laughed when he saw his expression of amazement. He was already in high gear and when he realized John was joking, they walked down the hall laughing and giving men orders.

Chapter 42

The room slowly came into focus from the blackness of a deep sleep. Sounds of medical machinery beeping and chirping to a nonsensical pattern filled her ears as she awoke. She tried to sit up and realized that her head still hurt, and laid back down. Looking around she saw her father and mother sitting at her side, together again. In her imagination she was a little girl again and they were a happy family, laughing together.

"Jessica!" called Melinda to her dozing daughter. "Sweetheart, over here!" she said again.

Jessica focused again on her parents. "Mom? Dad? I didn't die?" she asked hoarsely. "The virus?" she asked again.

"You'll be fine." Greg said as he gave her a sip of water from a cup and straw with ice in it.

"What about the virus?" she said as she hesitated to drink from the straw, remembering what her mother had told her before she got sick.

"It's OK. You are immune now." said Melinda.

Jessica took a drink. "Thanks Dad. Mom? I'm going to live?"

"Yes, honey. You'll be OK now." Melinda said with a smile. She squeezed Jessica's hand and looked into the eyes of her ex-husband. "We'll all be OK."

Chapter 43

Matthew Parker continued the momentum of his fall and rolled to his feet inches from his assailant. With a quick backhand to the left temple followed by a roundhouse to the head he completed his attack. Landing in a ready stance, he rested there for a moment and then stood erect and bowed his head. Arms at his side, he took a steadying breath and let it out slowly.

Matthew picked up the remote and turned off the music. 'My Generation' by the Who was silenced. He decided that before he showered he'd go for a swim. On his way to the pool he flipped on the radio.

"...somewhere in Arizona.

Our main story today of course is the President's announcement that Martial Law has been revoked some two months after the aerial spraying of the miracle nanobots. Across the country people are reporting no new cases of the deadly Manheim virus.

'I am pleased to announce that I am rescinding Martial Law Nation Wide. Our citizens have proven once again their resilience and character in the face of a devastating disaster.

This is thanks to the contributions of many people including Matthew Parker who invented the nanobot technology, Melinda Chase and her excellent team at the CDC who made the cure public, and of course Dr. Thomas Katz who brought them both together. Last but not least we can't forget Derek Manheim and his discovery of the meteor on which this terrible virus came to earth.'

That again was President George Bush speaking from the Nations' Capital. Melinda Chase of the CDC also says that the Army, Navy, Air Force and other military branches have joined forces under the control of the National Guard who will coordinate the sanitization of commercial and private property throughout the nation. In English this means that they will remove the dead from our cities and dispose of them in mass graves outside the city limits. She says there is no risk of disease spreading from the dead bodies. All bodies will be identified and numbered and a registry will be set up with the Federal Ministry of Health to help catalogue the dead for the benefit of the survivors.

Thanks to the broadcast of the Parker Cure, as it's now being called, our nation and the world are joining together to rebuild our communities.

It has also been reported that at the Northwest Medical Center in Issaquah, Washington that a commune of sorts run by a retired Lieutenant Colonel John Reed has also survived the disaster. What's so special about that? Christian Powers reports from our affiliate in Seattle.

'Survivors of the alien plague that devastated our nation are being found around the country in communes, but none like this one.

Lt. Col. John Reed rescued 112 people who beat the odds and survived against the alien virus, against looters and against cancer. Yes, that's right Cancer. I asked him what happened.'

'Well, we secured the building, took a count of survivors and twelve of them had cancer. We built the

Parker Cure device and used it on everyone against the virus and it worked wonderfully. Dr. Thomas Katz asked Matthew Parker for the programming to cure cancer, as he had originally intended. He obliged and all twelve are cancer free after receiving one treatment. It's really amazing.'

There you have it. The cure for the alien virus, and as a bonus, a cure for cancer has been found. Christian Powers, California Public Radio, Los Angeles."

Matthew dove into the pool at the deep end and started some laps. As he regulated his breathing and fell into an easy breast stroke, Matthew thought about Rebecca Forster. She had trusted him completely and her life had been stolen from her. Dr. Magee and Albert Jennings should pay for her murder, but who would care now? He thought.

Matthew continued his laps until he tired and headed for the shower.

Chapter 44

Albert Jennings smiled as he drove his Cadillac from Flagstaff towards Winslow Arizona along Highway 40. It had taken some convincing and another pile of money to have his precious Cadillac shipped from California.

It was another beautiful sunny day and he had the windows up and the air conditioning on. Albert found that with his heavy build and Greek heritage, the Arizona heat made him sweat profusely. It was something he hadn't considered when he planned his retirement to the small ranch house.

As he drove through Winslow, he picked up a tail. It was a black SUV. He hadn't seen it in town before and was suspicious. Albert didn't panic though, he had been followed before. He accelerated gradually to see if the SUV would do the same and when it did, he pushed the gas pedal to the floor. The 400hp v8 of the old car sprang to life and left the SUV behind.

Smiling to himself, Albert lit his stogie again. Foul blue smoke filled the car. Albert was putting the lighter back in his pocket, but dropped it accidentally. Cursing to himself, he reached down between his feet to get it, drifting off the road and onto the shoulder, almost losing control of the big car.

Regaining his composure he corrected the slide and gained the road again. The Black SUV was back. He couldn't see the driver with the reflection off the windshield. Albert accelerated again. There was really nowhere to go. The highway stretched into the distant horizon as straight as an arrow. His only hope was to outrun the SUV and turn off on the ranch road before its driver saw where he turned. He accelerated again and the Cadillac smoothly went 80, 90 then 100 miles an hour.

The SUV kept up until Albert reached 110, it felt to him like he was going 50. The quality of this vehicle and the weight to power ratio allowed his car to float down the highway, even at high speeds.

The SUV on the other hand was shaking like a stagecoach on a wagon trail. It hadn't been made for this speed and was becoming unstable at 95 mph, the driver backed off. It wasn't necessary to keep up, knowing what was ahead.

Albert saw his turn coming and slowed his Cadillac for the left turn onto the unnamed road to his ranch house. As he turned he looked back to his left and couldn't see the SUV through the heat waves coming off the highway. Smiling again he assumed he was safe.

The dirt road threw up dust behind his vehicle like a rooster tail on a race boat as he headed for the safety of his estate and pulled up to the house. When Albert got out of his vehicle but before he could close the door, four police cruisers came out from around his out-buildings with lights going and surrounded him. Officers jumped out and leveled their guns at him. "Hands in the air! Don't move!" yelled the sergeant in charge.

Albert smiled, raised his hands and said, "Officers, what seems to be the trouble? I'm sure we can work something out." He suggested and reached into his jacket. The officers took closer aim. "Eeeeeasy boys, just pulling out an envelope full of money!" he said and slowly pulled back his hand and showed them the open envelope full of green US currency. "See?" he said.

The officers were looking at the money and didn't notice Albert's other hand coming up with his handgun.

"I wouldn't mate!" said a familiar voice behind him accompanied by a click of a hammer being pulled back on a handgun. "That would be suicide, and you aren't the type."

Albert dropped the gun and turned to see Bobby Spears.

"'Allo Albert, fancy meeting you here at this nice place. Well, mate, these gentlemen have an even nicer place for you; room and board provided and plenty of space. Prisons are quite empty since the virus hit and there'll be room for the likes of you." said Bobby cheerfully, "Gentlemen?"

"Very funny Spears, I'll be out before days end. I've got contacts you could only dream of." said Albert confidently.

"Haven't you heard chum? More than half of the world's population is dead. I'd find it hard to believe if any of your buddies were still alive, the Good Lord Willing." Bobby offered.

Albert just laughed. "We'll see." He said.

Bobby frowned as he watched the officers cuff Albert and place him in the back of a cruiser, load up the others and drive out of the ranch house leaving a behind a cloud of dust. He owed Matthew Parker his life and this was just a partial payment.

Albert smiled with his cigar between his teeth and asked the officer in front, "Got a light?"

Chapter 45

The CH-46 Navy Sea King helicopter declared 'feet dry' as they crossed the beach at Antofagasta, Chile. The weather was clear and visibility excellent. The helicopter had been launched by the USS San Antonio that had been sent from the Naval Station in San Diego at the request of the President of the United States.

The Black Hawk followed the coastal range south from Antofagasta about fifty miles and turned inland. The Paranal Observatory was in the middle of nowhere, literally. The sandy expanse from which the mountain arose went for miles in any direction. The rainfall that had come so rarely had turned the desert roads to mud. A single dirt road led up the mountain to a plateau carved from the mountainside where the Observatory sat with stark white buildings set against the red of the desert landscape.

The helicopter began it's descent over the helipad swirling dust around the compound. Derek Manheim watched from the window of his lab with interest. "They are here KAMY." He said to the AI computer. "It's time for me to go."

"I understand Derek. Shall I go on standby mode?" asked KAMY.

"Do computers have feelings?" Derek thought that KAMY sounded a bit sad.

"No KAMY, stay active and watch the phone lines. We may need you again." answered Derek.

"OK. I will stay active. Thank you Derek! Will you call me?" KAMY asked sounding concerned.

"Of course KAMY, I'll check in on you. I have to go now." Derek said. He couldn't help feeling sad himself as he left. KAMY had been company for him for almost two weeks now. Without her conversation he probably would have gone insane. "Goodbye KAMY."

"Goodbye Derek." the computer replied.

Derek walked down the stairs and out the door into the brilliant sunshine and swirling dust. The Black Hawk rotors were almost stopped as he approached the landing pad. Then four masked men in black military issue Navy Seal uniforms jumped out of the helicopter and formed a line blocking his entrance. They all had MP5s pointed at him.

He stopped where he was, more than slightly intimidated by the display of weaponry.

A fifth man appeared in the door of the helicopter and jumped down to the ground. He was dressed in the same black outfit. He walked between and through the men and removed his mask.

"Top o' the morning to you son! Sergeant Connie Quinn at your service." He extended his hand and smiled warmly. "Derek Manheim?" Derek nodded. "The President says you need a ride!"

"Thanks! I sure do!" said Derek enthusiastically.

"A'right then Boyo, shall we?" Connie waved his hand towards the helicopter door, then raised his forefinger in the air and made a circle. The Black Hawk rotors started to wind up again as he said to his men, "Let's go boys!"

The men lowered their weapons and helped Derek aboard. With everyone in and secured, the Black Hawk helicopter lifted off in a cloud of dust. As it ascended and dipped towards the west and Connie asked "Do you want some coffee lad?"

Derek's eyes lit up and he said "Absolutely!"

Savoring the aroma of the hot coffee in the plastic cup he took a reverent sip. "Ahhhhh" he said. Derek watched the Paranal Observatory shrink in the distance as the helicopter headed for the coast and out to sea.

www.ingramcontent.com/pod-product-compliance
Lightning Source LLC
Chambersburg PA
CBHW071305170626
46809CB00001B/339